The Twelve Ways
of Christmas

SANDRA M. ODELL

The Twelve Ways of Christmas

SANDRA M. ODELL

Hydra House

Seattle, Washington

The Twelve Ways of Christmas

978-0-9848301-7-6 (print)
978-0-9848301-8-3 (ebook)
Library of Congress Control Number: 2012950075

Hydra House
1122 E Pike St. #1451
Seattle, WA 98122
http://www.hydrahousebooks.com/

Editor: K.C. Ball
Cover art and interior art: Lorn Cox
Cover design and interior design: Tod McCoy

First paperbound edition.

Printed in the United States of America.

For Doug

On the twelve days of Christmas my true love sent to me:

FOREWORD

What inspired *The Twelve Ways of Christmas*? Hope.

In 2011 I suffered a stroke and struggled to regain much of what I had lost. I couldn't write, in many ways couldn't think, and felt lost in a way known only to a scarce few. Months went by, and with them my hopes for the future. Writer's block and suicide rates haunted my dreams.

December came and with it the first niggling of an idea that rattled in my skull. A mechanical partridge singing in a pear tree, brass and copper sides, green velvet leaves. While putting away laundry one evening, I took the first steps towards redefining my abilities. If I couldn't write long, I could write short. Real short if need be. Write. That's what writers do. I'd been writing since I was six years old, had dozens of publication credits to my name, and at that moment decided I would not go down without a fight.

Finding motivation in the holidays, twelve days before Christmas I began to write the story of that mechanical partridge. Yes, *The Twelve Days of Christmas* refers to the twelve days between Christmas and the Epiphany, but I knew that if I waited for the calendar to catch up to my determination I might as well change my name to Hemingway and call it quits. So, for twelve days I wrote, edited, and posted a story a day to my website, a genre re-imagining of each of the lyrics. Partridge. Turtle doves. French hens. Calling birds. And no cheating. I didn't start a day early, I finished before midnight. I refused to give up. I wanted my words back, dammit!, and no pansy-ass stroke was going to take them from me without a fight.

The Twelve Ways of Christmas is the collection of those twelve stories. Science Fiction, Fantasy, Horror, Humor. Between these covers you will celebrate the holiday on a space station, say good-bye to a loved one on Christmas Eve, witness a gift that's good for the gander, scream at the bitter touch of Christmas ghosts, learn how not to clone your daughter for Christmas, even give a nod to the drummers bringing up the rear. These are stories not only of Christmas, but of the spirit of dreams that drive us to look beyond our world to ones just around the corner. Yes, they are Christmas stories, but not one of them is warm, fuzzy, or even remotely dashes through the snow. Some will sit beside you and share a coffee, maybe a joke. Others will grab you by the throat and not let you go until the sugar plums dancing in your head have moldered away. This is a collection of Christmas stories for someone not afraid to look out the window and wonder, if only for a moment, what lives in the tick of the clock between the Eve and the holiday.

I hope you are that person.

Home for Christmas

Amanda braced herself against the interior bulkhead and pounded on the door. "Lyson? How much longer is this gonna take?"

"Not much longer," came the reply, tinny and flat, from the speaker. "Almost there."

She sighed and hooked the toe of her boot into the secure point above the doorframe. "You heard him."

Byron scratched under the high collar of his coat. The motion pushed the Environmental Engineer into the padded wall. "All I know is, he don't let us in soon I'm going to crash out. Twelve-on shifts get old after a while, and I'm wiped."

"Any minute now," Charlie Lyson said.

Canned station air, flashing red and green lights, regular updates from Sagan IV's Central Hub with the occasional "Happy Holidays, folks" for the eight-hundred crew members thrown in for good measure. Not exactly how Amanda anticipated spending her first Christmas Eve stationside. Nothing made her happier than making the stationer cut, but not being dirtside for Christmas felt wrong. For the first time in eight months, the homesickness welled up strong enough, fast enough, that she would have gladly given it all up for the next drop boat home.

To keep the feeling at bay, she silently ticked off ways to spend the evening: read in her bunk; queue up for a call San Diego dirtside in case a line opened; work up a sweat in the half-G gym; wait until midnight Universal Time to open her precious Vosges Dark Chocolate bar on Christmas day, not much of a gift but all her mother could afford to send and all the more special for it.

Waiting with the other four members of third-shift

Environmental Controls for Lyson to pull off whatever Christmas miracle he had in mind didn't even make it to the top ten. Maybe even the top twenty, depending on whether or not the mess still had the tofu roasts sliced for snacking.

She adjusted her makeshift wig and hairnet, a salvaged bit of cargo-bond to round out her impromptu Victorian costume. Amanda had initially decided to pass on Lyson's invitation for a Christmas party—*"Come In Costume! Bring Ye Olde Holiday Cheer!"*—but Susie Xiang had wheedled as only she could do.

"It's Lyson, fer Christ's sake. He's got four more days and then he's dirtside bound," Susie had said two days ago, a wreath of THC smoke circling her head.

Easy for her to say. Susie hadn't seen Lyson's overdrawn cargo allowance. As the third shift records specialist, Amanda had no choice but to report Lyson to Chief Numaid when she finally sorted through the hidden numbers.

Some days she hated her job, but she could have been penalized pay or sent back dirtside in disgrace if she hadn't turned him in.

How had Lyson managed to get everything past the cargo regulators, anyway? What did he need with copper wire? Brass fittings and springs? Matching blue crystal growth? Organic soil? A micro-hybrid dwarf pear tree, for Sun's sake? He'd used double his eight station years of cargo allowance in just under four months. Yeah, he could build a sow's ear from two sprung gears and a silk purse, but a list like that was honest-to-Sun crazy.

"What's that got to do with anything?" Amanda had motioned for the pipe, taken a hit. The smoke settled into her lungs, seeped into her limbs with lazy insistence. Maybe she should have checked the THC modulation before toking after her bunkmate.

Nah.

Susie Xiang hiccupped. "Nobody wants to go back dirtside, right? This is his last hurrah. We're all he's got since ..." She motioned towards her gut.

Amanda had inhaled thoughts of Lyson—damn, this was some good smoke—and exhaled her longing for a genuine Christmas tree, and holiday lights under an open sky instead of strung along gray corridors. Even worse, her family had won the lottery to burn a genuine Yule log on Christmas Eve. No doubt everyone back home would gather around to cheer on the first match and toast the coming year while she approved spending chits and updated safety protocols.

"So?"

Susie Xiang had shrugged like only she could, riding the motion in a slow-ass-over ceilingward spin that did not quite complete itself. She'd looked over her left shoulder, bright pink hair fanning around her head in the null-grav. "It's Christmas."

Good point.

Now Amanda wore one of Susie Xiang's civilian lace shirts two sizes too small, and a haphazard array of skirts and hoops scavenged from the remnants of cargo tubes. Susie Xiang had whipped up a chimney sweep costume out of recycled rags and had smudged her face with powdered lubricant as a nod towards Environmental Workers of days gone by.

The rest of the team floated in a similar state of costume disarray in the center of the residential spoke. Byron dressed as a gentleman caller. Bruce Boy had snagged a white sheet somewhere and was dressed as an old-fashioned clergy, complete with an old-timer black protocol notebook for a dirtside bible. TepTep wore a top hat made from a spent respirator core, and the black undersuit from an EVA rig which Amanda didn't think had anything to do with Victorian times, but what the hell. Honest-to-Sun, optional clothing and effects were too expensive for crewmen to be choosers.

Now if Lyson would get it in gear before she decided to ditch the skirts and head for the chocolate.

The air duct between Amanda's legs came to life with a huff and a slurp of her skirts. "Taggit," she swore under her breath. Amanda positioned herself to the right to set her direction for the pull, while TepTep helped her gather handfuls of the colorful plastic.

"Hold on," TepTep said, "I think I—"

"Tenshun!" rapped a voice from below.

The crowd turned topside-up to attention and focused on the center of the corridor. First Shift Chief Faisal Numaid came up from the pass-thru, a security officer in his wake. Numaid put a hand up to stop his momentum against the designated ceiling above the tube.

"Isn't this a surprise?" he said drolly, hooking a foot into a secure point. "All dressed up for a party, hmmm?"

The security officer set himself one secure point farther up the wall, managing to look bored and attentive at once. The usually exuberant Susie Xiang turned slightly to the right and covered her chest with her arm. TepTep put his hat behind his back. Numaid looked Amanda up and down. Amanda couldn't decide if his smile had any genuine humor.

Coming to the attention of the "First Shift Shark" fell lower on Amanda's Christmas list than waiting for Lyson to get his act on straight. Please, oh please, oh please, don't let Numaid get a hair up his butt and try to pin any of this on her. All Amanda wanted was her chocolate and a solid ten of sleep. Her stomach flip-flopped as she crunched the fines that could be levied against her account should Sagan IV's command decide to ping her for Lyson's loony-tune spending spree.

She jerked her skirts out of the air duct, cringing at the sound of tearing plastic. Great. She'd have to clean that out before bedding down, another Christmas blow out.

"Not really, sir," she said when it looked like no one else would break the silence vac.

"Good," he said, "because I wasn't invited, and I'd hate to crash a party." He pushed off to the door and rapped three times. "Charlie, open up. It's time to have a little talk about your cargo charges."

Amanda's wrist unit beeped. She glanced down to find a flashing file marked with Numaid's designator. She cut an eye to the first shift chief, who looked at her then away. Amanda opened the file, and blanched. A writ of debt against one Charles W. Lyson Jr. and authorization to take said individual into custody.

From the frowns and sudden sweats, Numaid had sent the file to the others. TepTep looked at her, eyebrows on the rise. Amanda shrugged, hoping he believed she knew nothing about anything.

Lyson's voice came from the speaker. "Faisal, is that you?"

"One in the same, now open up," Numaid said. "I want a last look at your smiling face before we ship you off to debtor's prison for the rest of your dirtside days."

Now all of the others stared at her. Amanda looked at her feet. She'd done her job, that was all. None of this was her fault.

Yes, yes it was. What a crappy Christmas present, to send someone to debtor's prison. Maybe she could ditch her skirts and hide in the duct work until the next drop boat.

"Right on time." The door rolled open and Charlie Lyson poked the upper-half of his body out. He wore a gray wool cap, and a near perfect replica of a civilian dirtside dress coat complete with gold-stitched lapels and a sprig of something green and leafy in the topmost buttonhole. A copper wire mustachio perched between his pale nose and upper lip.

Lyson righted himself to match the common point of reference. "Come on in."

Numaid peered inside, hesitated, and cautiously pushed through the door. Following the smaller man's lead, Amanda went next. She stopped dead in the center of the entry. "Aside," Bruce Boy said in her ear. His foot in her back encouraged her to move the rest of the way in.

The room was dark save for the daily Christmas of Sagan IV's flashing lights indicating the floor. A pale yellow spotlight hung from the determined ceiling. The room's furnishings had been tucked into Lyson's sleep net and bundled in the far corner. In the center of the room sat a hard plastic cap out of which grew a meter-and-a-half tall tree. Rich soil clung to the roots and plastic; specks of dirt floated in the air.

Red and gold pears no longer than Amanda's thumb grew at null-grav inspired angles amidst leaves greener than any she had seen since arriving station-side. Cinnamon, orange peel, and the smell of growing things tickled her nose, mingling with childhood memories in the tears suddenly thick at the back of her throat.

"Oh my," she said in a bare whisper.

Byron pushed past her. "What's all the—Oh—"

Someone bumped into her back. Amanda pulled herself forward to give them all room in the cramped space.

"Everybody in?" Lyson said. "Close the door, close the door."

TepTep pulled the door down, swaddling them in shadow and pale gold. Eight bodies hung in null-grav.

Lyson toed back, and rubbed his hands together.

"Welcome one and all to the Charlie Lyson Christmas Extravaganza." He pulled a hip flask out of a coat pocket and presented it to Numaid.

Numaid looked from the flask to Lyson. "Is this ... a bribe?"

"Probably," Lyson said with a smile and a wink, "but could you at least wait until we're through here before you write me up?"

After a moment's hesitation, Numaid accepted the flask, sipped from the nipple, and passed it to Amanda. She sniffed, expecting brandy or some other dirtside luxury. Station juice. She sipped, passed the flask to Byron. Odd how the burn she'd disliked every other time now filled her with a warmth that kindled memories of her mother's Christmas Eve hot toddies, her father's one-finger of bourbon with a single ice cube.

"I suppose you're wondering why I called you all here." Lyson stroked his mustachios. "Yes?"

Caught in the moment, not knowing what else to do, Amanda nodded. So did the others, even Numaid and the security officer.

"Good." Lyson pushed off to the net of furniture where he extracted a small wooden box. He directed himself back to the tree, tucking the toe of his boot into the room's sole secure point. "I, um, I know I kept you waiting and all, but I just wanted to say, um ..." As he glanced at Amanda then Numaid, Lyson's cheeks flushed a dark rose, a startling contrast to his recent pallor. "I wanted to ... ah, to hell with it."

Lyson moved to the far side of the tree and turned his back to them. Amanda heard the box open, close, and then a faint winding of a spring. Someone tapped Amanda on the shoulder with the flask. She accepted, and sucked out the last few drops of liquid warmth.

Moments later, Lyson returned to where they

could see all of him, one hand cupped over the other. He smiled, a little sad, a lot proud. "I wanted to thank you folks," he said, voice cracking. He cleared his throat. "My contract's up and all, health being what it is, and I gotta go dirtside. You're some of the damn finest folks I know, and I wanted to thank you for eight of the best ... " He cleared his throat again. " ... the best damn years of my life. Merry Christmas."

Lyson opened his hands, and the partridge began to sing.

Worth more than eight-years-worth its weight in gold, the bird sat in Lyson's palm, pretty as could be, a tiny wonder of sheet metal, circuits, and wire, springs and blue crystal eyes. It called to Christmas in the soft spotlight, a clear, brittle song, sweet and poignant. It sang of snow and desert, of windy winter nights on the plains and the chill of Christmas morning in the cities. It sang of dirtside and stationside, inside and out, in clear, sweet copper tones.

The partridge wobbled to the edge of the big man's fingers, wings fluttering with the illusion of flight. He brought his hand to the tree and it hopped onto a branch where it clung with tiny brass claws.

Standing in shadows before the tree, surrounded by stationers, wet warmth separated from Amanda's lashes in tiny silver globes, taking her home to a place where Christmas shone in the system lights and in the eyes of an assistant engineer who did not want to leave.

Lyson caught her eye, mouthed, "It's okay."

A beep at her wrist. Amanda wiped away the tears and glanced at her wrist unit to find receipt of a file from Chief Numaid—Charles Lyson Jr.'s debt absolved and the costs absorbed by the station's emergency fund. Amanda attached her designator below Numaid's and closed the file.

Tourterelle Des Bois

I reached for the envelope on my grandmother's trembling chest. Boney fingers clutched the faded parchment. She opened her eyes and stared in my direction.

"*Non,*" she said, soft, succinct.

The word hung in the stale hospital air, the beeps and whistles and faint bells ringing flat beneath it. I took a hesitant step to the right so she could better see me. Her cataract clouded gaze shifted after me, drifted, fell away. Her hands, the hands that guided me down the lane when I learned to ride my bicycle, that covered and gently directed my own while I stirred dough for Christmas palmiers, were now palsied, skin-covered twigs. I hated the years in them. The sight of them served as a reminder that I could not save my grandmother from the shadows lurking in the encroaching dusty corners of her life.

I covered her hands with one of my own, both to offer comfort and to hide the spindly things from my sight. "I only wanted to put the letter away, Meme."

"I told you. I told you," my mother said bitterly from her perch by the window. "You are so much like your father."

Again, "*Non.*" Meme Eloise's eyes drifted shut. She gave a small, hiccupped snore around the hiss of the nasal oxygen. Her fingers remained curled around the letter, denying me my good intentions.

"Why do you even bother?" Mother said.

I straightened, exhaling a breath I had not realized I'd held. I turned to my mother. She wore intolerance and fatigue like badges of honor, features pinched to hold them in place. I could not recall her ever having looked otherwise, even when she served me plates of tiny salted chocolates—or grapes and thin slices of fresh charolais—after school.

Though they shared the same cheeks and chin, how different her features seemed from my grandmother's, now pinched with cancer. I felt compassion for one of them. "I only wanted to look at it again."

"It is a photocopy from some old magazine, nothing more," she said, staring at the gray clouds beyond the Clinique Saint-Georges. Her fingers strayed past her lips with the memory of a cigarette. "Nothing more."

I took a sip of coffee, and looked to the envelope gripped in Meme Eloise's hands, noting the silver script along the back flap, the tiny tear at the right corner. When she first showed me the letter some thirty-odd years ago, I found it incredibly old. Now, I wondered how her grip did not crumble it to dust.

"Meme always said it was a drawing."

"You are such the romantic, Alain." My mother laughed, a sharp, lonely bark. "Like your father. *Algérien stupide.*"

"And?"

She waved away the challenge. "She's a tired, old woman desperate for excitement, addled in the head."

Outside the door, nurses hurried to answer a distant, shrill alarm; outside the window, thunder coughed and prepared to open the sky in the velvet dark of *la veille de Noël.* We three huddled small and obsolete between the two. It was not the first time I'd felt that way since the surgeon's final diagnosis.

"The letter means something to her."

"There's nothing to it but fairytales and memories of the war."

I reached out and tenderly stroked Meme's silver white hair, thinking as I did that I might call in a beautician to wash and curl it if she made it through the night, perhaps color it Meme's favorite winter blonde, her one conceit. Was it too much to ask God for one more bright miracle, that Meme Eloise would wander the streets of Nice of an afternoon with nice hair, as she had so many times before? We would meet at Lu Fran Calin for coffee and croissants. I would tell her of my latest canvas, and she would share news of her garden.

"It brings her comfort," I said. "That's not so much to ask of a fairytale, is it?"

Mother snorted, and fished a stick of gum out of her purse. "*Fées*," she said, unwrapping the sugar-free pink wafer. And in a taut, caustic mockery of Meme Eloise's Paris childhood: "*Fées*."

That bit deep, and I said more sharply than I should, "She's dying. Why can't you let her even do that much in peace?"

She turned on me then, the woman who'd given me life rather than taught me how to live. Her wide brown eyes, so very much like mine, were at once poisonous and frightened. "So you can revel in the glory as the good son? Is that what you want?" Another laugh, not a pretty sound. "Your own bit of melodrama and heady tears like they show on American television?"

I gripped the bed railing to keep my place. She knew which buttons to push to bring out the worst in me. I felt the burn of my own venom behind my teeth, desperate for a voice. I swallowed it back. "No, so Meme can have a few moments to herself before passing on. The doctors' said she might not make it until morning."

As if forgetting herself, Mother's expression softened with the kiss of loss, and then tightened. She grabbed her purse. "I'm going for coffee," she spat as she stormed out the door. "Come find me when she's dead."

Thunder coughed once more, and it began to rain.

When I felt strong enough to move without

collapsing, I finished my coffee and followed it with a cup of water to wash the taste of the conversation out of my mouth. I splashed water over my face and hair. The chill followed the kinks of my tight curls to my scalp, a kiss of winter within the clinic's stifling comfort.

"Alain."

Meme Eloise sought and could not find me. I went to her, took her free hand, distressed by how dry her skin had become in the past two months. As a child, I'd sat beside her vanity while she'd rubbed lotion scented with violets and roses into her hands and feet to keep her skin soft. Once she'd let me apply the lotion for her, and I did so with devoted care. Now my heart filled with the smell, and my eyes with tears.

"Yes?"

"Alain," she said again, my name more breath than sound. "Do not ... hate her. I did not do very well by your mother."

Meme Eloise removed her hand from mine and slid a trembling finger under the flap of the envelope. She pulled out a piece of paper stained with tea, taped down the middle from my childhood excitement at being allowed to hold the page for the first time. She opened it, smoothed the paper on top of her comforter. "You see? He will ... come. Two turtle doves. Two beloveds. Then and now."

Captured in thin black lines and a gray-rose ink wash, two turtle doves nestled in a circle of holly and ivy, the berries bright red, the leaves a promise of spring. The left bird's head rested on the right bird's breast. As if to keep the snows edging the circle at bay, the right bird shielded the left with a protective wing. My grandmother ran a finger up the side of the paper to a precise point and moved inward to trace the birds, the feathered head and arch of wing, the berries and leaves and winter. As she followed her map of memory, I began to cry.

"On a night like tonight, he came, *la veille … de Noël*, and every year thereafter. Sometimes twice. Sometimes twice," she cooed, stroking the birds as if to give the feathers a bit of her fading warmth. "Such a handsome fellow."

I bent over her bed, transfixed by the telling. I was suddenly a boy again, sipping cocoa and nibbling just one more cookie during long winter nights when she told similar tales.

"During the war, the *Allemand*, oh, how they plagued him. My sweet, sweet bird." She brought the paper to her face and kissed the birds one at a time, her aged parchment lips leaving no mark. "During the occupation, we were … were allowed to celebrate the *Noël*, but our hearts were so grieved it was rare we put any faith in it." She smiled, closed her eyes. "But when he came for me, oh, it was magic. We once made love in a basement shelter. His hands on my body … "

I am a grown man and I blushed at the sudden warmth in her voice.

"Go on," I said when she'd fallen silent for too long. Hoping to stave off the coming silence? Perhaps.

She turned her head to the left without opening her eyes. "There is nothing more to it. He will come."

And she fell asleep once more, her long, thin fingers laced over the paper.

A watercolor picture of a *crèche* sat on the nightstand beside her bed, one of my recent works, painted just for her. Beside it, a tiny shoe, one of my baby shoes, filled with orange peel and hard candies. Shadows passed for the viewing along the walls of the dimly lit room, echoes of my grandmother's pallid vision, no replacement for family and friends she'd outlived, but all that she had anymore. Aside from myself, and her daughter, in the hospital cafe drinking coffee and thinking hateful thoughts.

I'd set the digital clock in the top drawer, denying the bright red flick and flash. Why couldn't I extract the time from those passing minutes and strain it through my grandmother's IV? Or feed her bits of my own life to give her an extra day, week, more?

Fairy tales, my mother would sneer, useless dreams to distract us from more important matters. Money. Responsibility. Priorities. My mother lived by those bitter words. Had she used them as weapons to drive my father away before my first birthday? They certainly would have framed my life if not for my grandmother's stories and tender attentions.

Thanks to Meme Eloise's generosity, I attended art school where my passion for color and line became my livelihood. I had my own gallery, my own studio, my own students that I nurtured in turn, all thanks to her. Now she lay dying, swaddled in wartime memories and delusions. What I wouldn't give for my mother's barbed sensibilities so I could cut out the pain and get on with my life. It had worked so well for her, why wouldn't I want to surround myself with lies of a happiness I could not feel?

Because I dared to love, and with loving came pain. Meme Eloise taught me well, the final chapter of her lesson presented as I sat beside her bed. I hoped my grandmother's turtle dove would come, if only in her dreams as she slipped away from me. I could do nothing more. She was dying, I could not stop it, so I sat at her bedside, listened to the rain, and cried.

The rain had no answers, nor did the muted cacophony of the dying.

In time rain reminded me of the coffee and water, and I stepped into the *toilette* to relieve myself, closing the door out of courtesy and habit. When finished, I stepped out to find a man in scarlet and green standing with a young woman by Meme's bed. I did not recognize him. His hair and beard were a moonlit white, his eyes the blue of spring. The woman could have doubled for a younger version of my grandmother in a winter white shift and ivy green cloak reminiscent of a photograph Meme Eloise kept on her mantle.

Startled and suddenly uncertain—had I entered the room next door by mistake?—I opened my mouth to apologize. The man made a gesture, and I could not move. My legs were stone, the breath thick as lead in my chest.

The woman put a hand over his. "No more, my bird," she said, and turned to smile at me. "Alain, my heart."

I struggled within my invisible prison, my heart hammering against my frozen breath, and then the woman with winter blonde hair stepped away from the man to reveal a life-sized doll of twigs and muslin laying in the bed. The woman touched the man's hand again and I could move. I drew a breath, grateful, angry, and confused.

"Do not be afraid," she said.

I staggered forward a step, caught myself, and approached the bed. The figure of twigs and cloth lay very still, the paper on its ersatz chest blank, the turtle doves gone. I turned to the woman, reached out and touched her arm. "Meme?" I said, my voice a bare whisper, too astounded to doubt.

Meme Eloise, younger and more beautiful than I had ever known her, smiled up at me. "Alain." She took my hand and turned me to face her companion. "This is my bird, Nicolas."

Though his eyes were guarded, the man smiled and sketched a slight bow.

"But ... but ..." I looked from the doll on the bed to the young woman. "How have ... What did ..."

She laughed my grandmother's laugh. "He came for me, just as he promised."

The man, I could not say his name for doing so would have shattered the magic of the moment, brought her hand to his lips. "I did not mean to keep you waiting, but time is, well ..." He made an off-handed gesture that gathered decades and tossed them away.

Meme Eloise, my beautiful Meme. I did not want to look at the thing on the bed; the young woman shone with a light all her own. "What now?" I finally said.

My grandmother stepped to the man's side. "And now we must be off before the nurses come in for their rounds. Nicolas has promised me a sleigh ride, and then ..."

She looked at him with a smile and arched brow.

The man pressed the back of her hand to his lips a second time. "And then," he agreed.

I felt six-years old again, listening to Meme Eloise promise *"You'll understand in time, Alain,"* when I did not understand the reasons behind her smiles or tears.

She touched my cheek, bringing me back to the hospital and the rain. "You were such a splendid child, Alain. *Merci.*"

I pressed my lips to her wrist in silent praise of the vitality of her pulse. "Thank you. But ... "

"You will explain this to your mother, yes?"

I looked to the doll of twigs, the blank paper that once held a sketched ink dream brought to vibrant life. "What do I tell her?"

"Tell her ... tell her I love her very much. *Non.*" She frowned, at me, at herself. "*Non*, show her you love her. Something I could never do."

"I ... Yes." I nodded. "I will do my best."

I turned to the man with the spring blue eyes, the man I could not name but knew in the depths of my heart. "You will take care of her?"

He considered me for a moment, then smiled. "*Oui.*"

I did not recognize his accent, but the sentiment was genuine.

Meme Eloise and I embraced. She felt warm and vibrant in my arms, and for a moment I could not bear to part with her, but she gently separated herself from me. The man, her turtle dove, put an arm around her waist. "Good-bye, Alain," she said, and with a smile they disappeared in a sparkle of snow.

A shrill emergency alarm sounded from my grandmother's bedside where the doll lay still, not breathing. From a world away, *chant de Noël* colored the early morning dark, and I found I did not feel sad at all.

A Free-Range Panic at Alanda Farms

AP News Service (AP): Chaos ensued at Alanda Organic Farms & Restaurant early this morning when three French hens stormed the kitchen demanding to be served as coq co vin for Christmas dinner instead of as buttermilk fried chicken with an apricot balsamic reduction.

"I was shredding cabbage when they bust through the door crowing, 'Viva la coq co vin!' in this really cheesy French accent, I mean, Jerry Lewis French," said Marjorie Broughton, kitchen manager. "All our meat is free-range, but this was just too much, you know? And they would have crisped up so nicely, too."

Ms. Broughton said she was hen-pecked into a corner by the two Houdan while the Maran pelted her with pearl onions and crimini mushrooms when the chickens could not find the burgundy.

"I would never have used crimini," she said, in tears.

Afterwards, a brood of roosters tried to drown her in a pot of California red wine with three bay leaves, two cloves of garlic, and a quarter teaspoon of fresh ground pepper. The nationality of the roosters is unknown at this time.

Sheriff's deputies negotiated for the release of Ms. Broughton and two other wait-staff employees earlier this afternoon. The hens have not been found.

One deputy, speaking off the record, says the authorities believe the chickens may have escaped when they realized local officials planned to butcher and eat the hens after the stand-off was resolved.

Authorities report that upon hearing of the chickens demands for culinary predetermination, the cows staged a sit-in at one of the guest houses.

"It is every cow's right to be cooked in the manner of his or her choosing," the cows wrote, in a statement presented to the Leibowitz family later that afternoon. "And we insist that we be dry-aged and served with a light au poivre sauce and a glass of complementary Bordeaux Pomerol."

Eye-witnesses reported that the cows wore sandwich boards that read "Respect The Beef And The Beef Will Respect You", and "Just say Moo to the Hindu." According to roosters uninvolved in the kitchen incident, the cows did not fire first and reports to that effect are duck-circulated PR.

Ephram Leibowitz, owner and manager of Alanda Organic Farms & Restaurant, declined to comment on today's dinner menu uprising. He remains sequestered with his wife and four children. Upon hearing that the pigs were measuring themselves for wood smokers, Rabbi Biram of Isreal Beit Knesset, friend of Mr. Leibowitz, told the press, "Ephram is a good Jewish boy. What should he know about cooking pigs?"

Alanda Farms remains in flames, and has been cordoned off by authorities. A contingent of ducks was last seen with a gas heater and a crate of orange juice concentrate, headed to near-by Lake Omaghan where fish were reported out of the water, demanding to be poached with lemon and dill. Crisis management teams urge all diners to remain inside and keep away from the broilers until further notice.

To Speak of Metal Men and Birds of War

On the first day of the end of the world, Lieutenant Archimedes Phillips drinks stale water from a canteen cup, and bleeds. "If the bullet don't kill me, the lead will, huh, Tokker?" He coughs, draws a harsh breath. "Tokker?"

The little metal man finishes dressing the lieutenant's belly wound with a tincture of congealing mold and an oily rag. "Of course, Lieutenant Phillips," he says from the speaker in his chest. He drops the rag in his combustibles pouch. "May I take the cup?"

"How many times do I have to tell you to call me Ark?" The lieutenant struggles to sit straighter. Like a barbed viper, the pain curls through his gut. "Hoooo shit ..."

Tokker waits until the spasm passes. "Yes sir, Lieutenant Phillips. I have laudanum if you would care for it."

"I'm fine, fine. I just ... "

The Lieutenant's attention wanders to the west, to the *Alexander Hamilton*. Stuttering con trails circle the dirigible, halos of spite against dishrag gray clouds. "Y'think ... do you think they're going to make it home?"

Tokker gives the scene as much of his attention as he can. Given Lieutenant Phillips' condition, he must watch the surrounding hillside for scavengers or enemy troops. "If the gunners can keep the Reich squad at bay, yes."

Saffron and gold blossom near the aft of the airship. The *Alexander Hamilton*, most decorated vessel of the North American Fleet, slows and lists starboard, but does not stop.

The silence of war engulfs the field, no mice or

birds to disturb the near-by remnants of a ten-man expeditionary team, the core of a failed fifty-man insertion force. Too soon, shots crack open the stillness. Tokker swivels his head around and extends his sight. In the distance, men and women approach with rifles, skinning knives, and bags; gaunt reminders of the hardships of war seldom seen from the dirigible decks.

"Scavengers, Lieutenant Phillips, most likely locals. They will not be sympathetic to your state. We must get you to a place of safety."

"Damn." Phillips sighs, rolls onto his side with a grunt. He clutches the grass to keep from falling off the ground. "Let's go."

Tokker stands. "Yes, Lieutenant Phillips."

They reach a copse of trees far enough from the killing ground to no longer be of interest to local vermin. Through the screen of branches they watch the *Alexander Hamilton* go down.

Phillips closes his eyes. "You're an awful liar, you know that, Tokker?"

Tokker's eyes shutter—close-open, snap-snap— capturing the dirigible tumbling to the earth, a fiery angel with broken smoke wings. The image is burned onto a piece of silver-plated copper behind his eyes, exposed to a hint of mercury vapors, and slid to the bottom of the photographic deck. "Yes, Lieutenant Phillips. I am sorry, Lieutenant Phillips."

"I'm not going to make it."

"You will, Lieutenant Phillips."

Phillips drops his chin to his chest. "I should have gone down with them."

"There was no way for you to make it to the rescue flotilla, no way for them to wait for you." Tokker does not remind Phillips that Reich forces shot down the flotilla before it reached the Hamilton. "You are the lone surviving crewman of the *Alexander Hamilton*, and must now husband your strength to make it to Chievres for your report. Command will be expecting you."

Once more they settle to silence. Phillips lays with his eyes closed. Tokker keeps watch at the tree line for movement.

"You think she remembers me, Tokker?" the lieutenant says eventually.

While he continues to keep watch, the metal man turns his torso one-hundred-eighty degrees so his speaker faces Phillips. "Of course."

Phillips snorts. The sound breaks apart in a cough that leaves him on his side, clutching his gut. Tokker scrambles over, brass bits and knobs clattering. "Lieutenant Phillips? Here, here, sir, let me."

Together they roll Phillips onto his back. His abdomen is starting to swell. Tokker presses makeshift bandages torn from a dead man's shirt over the wound to help staunch bleeding; he unbuttons the lieutenant's trousers to ease the pressure. The metal man props Phillips' head on the lieutenant's gear sack, and feeds him small sips of laudanum until the man pushes the bottle away.

Phillips' face is ashen and slick with sweat, blood and spittle caked at the corners of his mouth. "Bernadette was some fine woman, but she don't remember me," he says when the laudanum begins to take hold. "What's a Belgian woman want with a black man from Tennessee, anyway? Mapping intelligence officer. I draw pictures is all."

Tokker cannot answer this, so he continues bathing the lieutenant's head with a damp cloth.

Finally: "Gimmee a bird, Tokker."

This the metal man can do. He fishes the keys out of the drawer beneath his speaker, four keys with the same teeth and different heads: diamond; club; spade; heart. He presents them to Phillips, and rotates his torso.

Phillips inserts the diamond key into the top right of four doors in Tokker's back. He turns it to the right, grits his teeth, and breaks off the key head. The door swings open, and with shaking hands he removes a bird of snow white gears.

"C'mere, birdie." Phillips' words are slurred with the weight of sleep.

The bird rests easy in Phillips' hands. The lieutenant licks his lips and whispers to the bird. Finished, he kisses the top of the bird's head and opens his hands. The calling bird rests still as can be for a moment before it spreads its wings and flies off, out of the copse into the early afternoon.

Phillips watches past the point where the bird can be seen. "You go on and find her, birdie. Tell her Archimedes sends his best. Go on now." And softer: "Don't remember me, don't need me."

Sleep takes the lieutenant.

Tokker waits until dusk before leaving the trees to hide any sign of their tracks. Afterwards, while Lieutenant Phillips mutters and groans in his sleep, Tokker returns to his watch at the tree-line.

On the second day of the end of the world, Reichmann foot soldiers scour the area for materials and intelligence.

Tokker creates a camouflage of leaves and branches over Lieutenant Phillips, crushing berries and pine cones to cover the stench of the man having soiled himself in the night. The metal man disconnects his own legs, covers them with leaves and wood boles. They are now a stump. He pulls himself into the branches above the lieutenant, hooks a branch above him and tucks it under the branch below, creating a screen no more or less natural than the after effects of a windstorm. He closes off his respiratory valves, damps his internal furnace, and turns off his eyes. Tokker tips his head back until it can't been seen from ahead of, or directly below, the tree, creating a silhouette of a large bird's nest or wad of leaves caught in the upper crook of the trunk.

The Reichmen are precise in their line. They step in time, coiled stainless steel springs bringing boots up, setting them down in exact measure, far superior mechanics compared to anything the Allies have yet to develop. Massive heads swing from side to side, guided by loyalty generated with careful gear-and-gap timing, nominally controlled by human brains of lesser intelligence housed somewhere in the torso.

The Reichmen approach the copse in a wall of spring and sinew, dark, heavy bricks that move like men. The wall splits into three, the masses to go around on either side, four soldiers to search the trees.

Tokker hears the quartet spread out. As they move through the trees, pushing aside the undergrowth in their search, he feels echoes of the heel-toe rumble of the iron twins, Berlin and Prague. For what are they searching? A mapping intelligence officer? Someone with intimate knowledge of Allied movements and environmental expectations? Perhaps.

Lieutenant Phillips whimpers.

Everything stops. The world is silent, the moment cast in amber. Tokker does not move. Below, servos whir, gears turn, joints click to the right and left, amber moments split.

Tokker hears metal retract and other metal slide into place, followed by the unmistakable sound of a gun safety being disengaged. A machine gun in place of an arm? As they probe through the undergrowth, the Reichmen do not speak in words; the occasional click and hum suffice. Tokker understands.

[Stop. I heard something.] [Where?] [Not certain. Come this way.]

Heavy steps from the right, the thrust and crumble of a bayonet probing the undergrowth from the left. Do they have infrared? Can they detect the differences in the foliage?

Tokker feels along the overhead branch for a cluster of leaves, breaks it off. He throws the leaves away from Lieutenant Phillips. The cluster lands in the brush, and there is a sudden chittering and a scurry of little claws.

[There.] [A squirrel.] [I see it. Move on.]

Linear thinking. It ensures loyalty, but does not promote understanding.

Steps move away, grow faint. Tokker counts a slow one-hundred before stoking his furnace with combustibles. The smell of burning blood sifts through the branches. In time, he climbs down and carefully cleans the leaves off the lieutenant's face. The man is slack-jawed and sweaty, asleep. Tokker leaves him covered; the detritus will keep him warm.

He sits beside Lieutenant Phillips, thinking deep thoughts, not his typical forte; he usually acts after others decide. Would he? Could he? Making his decision, he reattaches his legs and then selects the second key, the club key. More problematic is finding the means of securing it in a near-by trunk so he can maneuver himself onto it, but Tokker does, and then drops to the ground to snap off the head. With the top left door open, a bird tumbles out. He presses against the tree to close the door.

The metal man carries the bird with silver gears to the far side of the trees, stroking and tapping the bird's throat and sides as he goes. The bird is still in his hands. At the edge of the trees, Tokker searches the ground for tracks, looks into the distance, tapping, tapping, tapping. Finally, he releases the bird into the air. It flies directly west without a sound.

Tokker walks back to the lieutenant and wets a cloth to bathe his brow.

On the third day of the end of the world, Lieutenant Phillips' fever breaks. His abdomen is like that of a pregnant woman, swollen and hard, and he spends much of the morning retching up bile and the few sips of water he managed to swallow earlier.

"Why did you sign up?" he says, the words faint and breathy.

Tokker holds a pot of tea to steep over a tiny fire. He does not feel heat, nor the chill of the stiff breeze blowing through the trees. "Sign up?"

"You know, join the Air Army."

"I did not join. I was built to serve as an officer's attendant, assigned first to Fort Charleston, then as part of your billet on the *Alexander Hamilton*."

Lieutenant Phillips peers at him. He shifts, winces. Every breath steals a bit of strength, every movement a few seconds of life. "Made you to serve."

"Yes, Lieutenant Phillips."

"No." Lieutenant Phillips closes his eyes, perhaps dozes for a time. "I joined as part of a college scholarship. My momma was so proud of me. Haven't seen her since this whole war began. My first, my first Christmas on the *Hamilton* she sent me a box of shortbread and a picture ... a picture of her and my daddy they took at one of them booths at the county fair." And later: "What do you want to be when you get out?"

"Sir?"

It takes time for Phillips to answer. "Get out of the

Air Army. What are you going to do?"

Tokker considers the question. "I do not think I can leave the Service."

The lieutenant scowls. "Why not?"

Tokker shrugs in the fashion he has seen humans do. "I am an officer's attendant."

"That's like ..." He coughs, squeezes his eyes shut, opens them when he can. "... like me believing everybody who said I couldn't go to school for being black ... and black's all I was ever going to be."

The argument makes no sense to Tokker, so he shrugs a second time.

"You know I'm right," Phillips says.

"Yes, Lieutenant Phillips."

The lieutenant stares at him with brows drawn down and a heavy scowl.

Tokker says, "Would you like some tea? It will help ease your throat."

"Bird," Phillips says. "Get me ... a bird."

Tokker hands Phillips the keys and puts his back to the lieutenant.

Phillips stares at the spade key, at the top doors with the locks plugged by the remnants of their own keys. "I used two?"

The question is nearly lost in the sudden breeze, the rattle of leaves. The sun has started to set. The night will be cold.

"No, you only used the first bird. I used the second yesterday."

"Why?"

Tokker considers his answer for eight seconds and an autumn breath of leaves. "I sent a report to Chievres about the Reichmen and the *Hamilton*. And your condition."

"Did that for me, huh?"

Tokker nods.

Phillips stares at Tokker for a time. "Thank you," he says, barely above a whisper. He shifts, grimaces, holds up the keys in a shaking hand. "I don't, um, don't think I can …"

"Simply insert the key and turn it. I will do the rest."

Phillips does, and Tokker does, and soon the charcoal-geared calling bird sits in the dying man's hands. Phillips touches the beak with a trembling finger. "I miss my momma so much," he whispers, and begins to cry. "Miss her something fierce."

"No, Lieutenant Phillips, no. Do not cry. Have some tea, it will help your throat, it will … "

Phillips knocks the cup away. "Don't want no fuckin' tea!"

The defiance costs Phillips much. He lays still, chest clutching at breath, staring straight ahead. "Something fierce," Phillips says, and brings the bird to his mouth. He whispers, stops, adds a last few words, and releases the bird. The calling bird circles twice above the trees before flying off to the south and west.

Tokker retrieves the cup, wiping out the last bits of tea, returns it to the mess kit.

The setting sun has turned the leaves to shadows when Phillips says, "Laudanum?"

Tokker presents the slender brown bottle, ready to administer the drug in small sips, but Phillips takes it from him. The dying man's dark face is a blot of ink in the shadows, blurring eyes and nose, the red and white notes of his mouth. Before the metal man can stop him, Phillips empties the bottle in two ragged swallows. He coughs and gags behind closed lips, swallowing a third time.

"Lieutenant Phillips, that was not wise," Tokker says, gathering the bottle and stopper.

Phillips smiles, pats the metal man's side. "Call me Ark."

On the fourth day of the end of the world, Archimedes Phillips dies. He leaves with the wind, eyes open in the early dawn.

Tokker arranges the dead man in a comfortable position, sticks his tongue back in his mouth, closes his eyes, not that it matters now. He collects the gear sack, the lieutenant's comb and watch, the picture of Mr. and Mrs. Phillips smiling at the camera, waving to their son stationed on board the glorious *Alexander Hamilton*.

He builds a small fire from scraps in his combustibles pouch and makes a cup of tea in case Lieutenant Phillips wakes thirsty. He will, of course, not wake. Tokker knows this. Still, the tea steeps. He sits and thinks.

At mid-day, he releases the fourth calling bird with the heart key, black gears and yellow crystal eyes. He carefully places the ring with the four broken keys in the breast pocket of Lieutenant Phillips field jacket.

Tokker sits with the bird in his lap, hands unmoving against its metal feathers. He has never been to Tennessee, never been to a jazz club. Jazz clubs do not admit metal men. He once heard Lieutenant Phillips singing in the shower, *Carolina Baby* and *Swing Low, Sweet Chariot*. Tokker has never tried to sing.

He brings the bird up and whispers at length before releasing it on the dead man's chest. The calling bird does not fly away.

Tokker stands and begins to walk west, to Chievres, and then Tennessee.

Behind him, in the copse of trees, the calling bird begins to sing:

Sandra M. Odell

Swing low, Sweet Chariot,
Coming for to carry me home;
Swing low, Sweet Chariot,
Coming for to carry me home.

T'is the Season

I spot the monk reading on a bench at the mall, and from the inattentive scurry of the holiday shoppers I am all but certain I am the only one who does. How they miss those saffron robes I have no idea, but they do and I am.

Merry Kwanristmaskah and all.

Knowing Jill, my editor, will love a few shots of his unhurried solitude for our Christmas spread, and my checking account the extra cash, I glance at my watch and compare the time against the holiday schedule spinning in my head. Burt expects me at his son's birthday party cum Christmas extravaganza by 3-ish, and then I am supposed to meet Ken and what's-her-name—Shirley—for a getting-to-know-the-fiancé dinner. I might be able to make this work. I only have to buy a couple of something cute, which shouldn't take too long.

I take a chance the monk won't go anywhere, hurry out to the car for my camera bag, and brave a second run through the crowds to reach him.

I'm in luck. He hasn't moved. I approach with personal deference, and a professional eye. "Excuse me?"

He looks up and smiles. Thai or Cambodian, I decide, bald, tiny, a mole on the back of his left hand, in that eternal Asian span of age between sixty and six-hundred, wrinkled in all the ways that speak of a life lived at peace with itself.

"Yes?"

Perhaps it's a pause in the insistent Christmas carols, but I find myself smiling back. I present my card—**Olivia Miller. Photography, Portraits, Every Day Life**. I echo everything in print, finishing with, "And I wondered if I could take a few pictures of you reading, Brother, um …?"

"Choon," he says with a slight bow of the head. "No title, not any more. Just Choon."

He looks like southeast Asia, sounds like south Chicago. "Choon, then."

His smile widens, and so does mine.

I step back and unzip my case, considering lighting, exposure, focus. I want Choon in sharp relief, but what about the background? I like the thought of …

"If you will allow me to present you with a thank-you gift when you are through," he says.

That tips me out of my photographer's frame. "Pardon?"

At that he laughs, high and musical. I think of waterfalls and temple bells. "A gift. Nothing too ostentatious, I promise."

It's the first time I've ever heard someone from south Chicago roll their tongue around "ostentatious".

I frown and put my case on the bench beside me.

"I'm sorry. I don't have any cash on me and I only want a couple shots."

The monk settles back on the bench, hands in his lap. "Certainly."

Okay, am I supposed to pay him or just take pictures? When he doesn't hold out a change can or credit card machine, I figure everything will be okay, and get my camera ready.

I expect to defend my position from the crowd, but the people move around me without a hitch, as if they don't want to miss out on a sale of shoes with matching key protector, water bottle, purse, pouches or something. I hate holiday crowds, they're a drag. They bring me down and down and down. If the holidays don't involve guilt, they take money, and as a self-employed photographer, I have plenty of the former and none of the latter.

"What are you reading?" I say to fill the relative silence of checking lighting and exposure.

Choon rests the tips of his fingers on the open pages. "*The Five People You Meet In Heaven*."

I've heard about the book, but haven't read it. "Is it any good?"

He cocks his head to the side. "There are many things to consider."

I laugh and take a step back, almost bumping into a young woman hurrying down the ramp. As fluid as you please, she moves out of my way and hurries along without a backwards glance, chattering on her cell phone all the while. "Okay, then. Keep reading. I only want a couple of shots."

Choon lowers his attention to the small red book and, honest to Groucho Marx, begins to read.

When you ask a model to do something specific—read a book, open a box, look out a window—too often they only mimic the action and don't embody it. Choon doesn't happenstance glance at the page, he find the line where he left off and picks up reading. There's no other way to say it, he inhabits the act of reading. That fast, the book becomes his world. I can tell, and so can the camera.

All told, I probably shoot for three minutes. Jill will have a field day with these. I imagine an even larger bonus, extra assignments, my own giant cookie. When I finish, I sit beside Choon and go through the shoot, a courtesy for his kindness. He seems fascinated, leaning in close for a better look while I scroll through the shots.

"You have a wonderful sense of perspective," he says.

I shrug. "Thanks. Patience, practice, and more patience is all."

Choon touches the side of my camera the way he touched the pages of his book. "Of course. It is the knowing eye."

If he says so. I pack up my camera and check the time. So long as the maddened throng behaves, I can buy my Christmas bribe and make it out with enough time to get myself a coffee before the party. "Thanks for sitting for me. I really appreciate it."

"You are most welcome," he says, head bobbing. I prepare to stand when he adds, "Please. Your gift."

Right, right. He has something for me. "Sorry. I forgot all about it. Really, you don't have to ..."

"Please. You would honor me with your acceptance."

He doesn't offer up any guilt. I take an extra helping out of habit. "Sure."

Using what looks like a braid of dark hair for a bookmark, Choon sets the book aside and produces a small muslin bag from his robes, maybe the size of one of those bags of Christmas coal candy. From this he pulls a simple gold ring which he presses into the palm of my right hand. "For you."

I frown, closing my hand enough to flip the ring

over. No markings or designs, no karat mark inside, but with the depth of color and heft that make me think it is solid gold, not plated. I hold it up to the light. "Oh, no, I couldn't." I shake my head and try to hand the ring back.

"I have five rings. Yours is the third."

That makes no sense. Something from the book, maybe, or a bit of clever holiday word play. "It's lovely, and I appreciate the thought, but I can't accept it." I laugh. "It's worth, oh, I don't know, more than a hundred sittings."

Hands in his lap, Choon is a still pool of serenity in the ebb and flow of the crowds. "Sometimes when you sacrifice something precious, you're not really losing it. You're just passing it on to someone else."

I frown. "What?"

The little monk in saffron smiles, and gestures to the book beside him. "Wisdom from the book."

The whole third ring business must have come from the book. Feeling odd and a little uncomfortable, I set the ring on his knee. "I'm sorry, but I can't. I mean, I didn't do anything to deserve this."

"You did," he says. "You asked to take my picture."

Scratching the back of my head beats out wringing my hands in frustration. "But that was paying attention to you, which is bad since you're Buddhist and all, right?"

"No, you were attentive to the moment. The third ring is now yours."

"Oh, come on." Why am I arguing with him? Why don't I just walk away? "This isn't a Christmas present. You're not even Christian."

"Neither are you."

Good point. I'm agnostic, flirting with atheism at this time of year. His calm assurance of faith gets under my skin. "And?"

He bobs his head. "You are here as am I."

"What's that got to do with anything?"

"Everything and nothing," Choon says, and inclines his head.

Choon looks at me, takes in everything about me: my ponytail; my lack of make-up because I overslept; my second-hand sweater with the missing third button from the top. The river of people flow around us, our bubble of calm, and I have a terrible thought, one of those thoughts that claws its way up from my belly and catches hold of the breath in my throat.

Does that woman pushing the stroller see us and then look away, or does she not notice us at all? What about the guy with the green backpack, and Sears bags on his arm? Did he mean to move around us, or is he compelled to do so without realizing we are here? Do they see us? Only a few minutes ago I thought it odd that I was the only one to notice Choon sitting on the bench with a book on his lap. A book about dead people.

"Are you ...?" I swallow and try again. "Are you dead?"

He shakes his head once. No.

The next question clings to the back of my throat, and I fight to ask. "Am I?"

Choon stares at me.

I begin to shake, thoughts of those things I knew I shouldn't have done through the years crowding my chest. Pushing Veronica out of the oak tree in the back yard to see if she'd land on her feet; she broke her ankle. Shoplifting The Cars "Candy-O" from Hillmont Music at 14. A one-night stand with Avery's brother a week after my 22nd birthday; Avery was gone a day later. Acts that don't make me a bad person, but when flensed from my life and knotted around my throat, I suddenly can't breathe.

The monk stares at me in compassionate silence.

Words catch in the tangle of fear. I cough them free. "Say something. Please."

Choon leans close to me and, in a whisper, says, "Do not speak unless it improves on silence." He looks left and right. "Which is long hand for no, I don't think you're dead."

My bones turn to water and I all but collapse into him. I have the sudden urge to piss my pants.

Choon allows me to lean against him for a time before carefully shifting away so straightening looks like my idea. I feel light headed, nauseated, hot and cold, miserable and giddy. If I was more physical, I'd punch him. "I, uh, wow."

He inclines his head. "You're welcome."

I feel fire in my cheeks. "I don't know what to say. You must think I'm an idiot."

"I have come to understand there is no reason to wait until one's death to recognize those who make a difference in one's life." Choon collects the pouch and book, stands.

For such a small man, he takes up all of my vision, a precise moment of awareness, consciousness, with a shaved head and slender hands. He presses those hands palm-to-palm before him and bows from the waist.

"A pleasure making your acquaintance, Ms. Olivia Miller."

Like a fish coming to the surface of the water, or a leaf falling from a branch, he joins the crowd. I see the ring on the bench beside me. I pick it up, ready to give it back, but the monk in bright saffron robes has blended with the crowd and is gone. I stand at the top of the shallow ramp, alone.

No, one of five, and not alone at all.

Good for the Gander

From the kitchen came a brittle CRUNCH, then the expected "Ewww!"

Warren groaned and sank into his chair. "All right, all right! I'll take care of it."

Before someone could hand him yet another broken egg or gooey towel, he went to find Burt where he expected, at the snack table in the den picking pretzels out of the Chex Mix.

By the portly man's side, an African Brown goose pecked at crumbs on the carpet. The goose paused in its forage, honked and laid an egg the size of the fist Warren wanted to wrap around the fool bird's neck. The other guests kept to the edges of the room, except for Sherman who had enlisted the aid of a four-quart soup pot to collect the as yet unbroken eggs scattered over floor and furniture.

"Burt, we gotta talk, man," Warren said.

His friend looked up with bleary, bloodshot eyes. Warren couldn't say how, but Burt looked worse now than he had when he arrived at the party less than an hour before. "What's up?"

Warren motioned towards the balcony. "Let's get some air."

Burt sighed and grabbed a cold St. Pauli's Girl around the waist. "Sure," he said, and Warren led him out to the balcony while the rest of the partygoers pointed and whispered. The African Brown followed them out, its dewlap swaying beneath its chin.

Bright strings of Christmas lights flashed and blinked from the surrounding balconies, counterpoint to the stream of late night Miami holiday traffic far below. *Rock And Roll Christmas* drifted up from a lower floor with insistent electric cheer.

Warren turned to the guests cornered by two Roman Tufted geese exploring the ashtrays and overturned drinks. "Listen, do you mind? A little privacy?"

The men and women hurried off the balcony, the last woman crushing a freshly laid egg with her four-inch heel. She grimaced and hopped over the threshold while one of the men closed the door behind her.

Warren exhaled a puff of air and rubbed his face with both hands. "Man, I'm sorry. I really thought this could work, but … "

Burt took a long pull from his beer. He kicked a goose from between his feet. "S'alright. You did your best."

Warren winced. "I really am sorry, it being Christmas, but, I mean … "

He gestured at the ground where the remains of a dozen or more eggs had been smeared on the cement, and another half dozen pristine, whole eggs pushed against the outside wall of the condo.

A Canada Goose passed through the closed glass door and onto the balcony. Warren pointed to the goose.

"And that?" he said. "What the hell am I supposed to do about that? That's not right. And, I mean, I've never even seen pictures of these geese, I don't know what they are and somehow I know what they are."

Burt's shoulders slumped. "Yeah, I know." He finished his beer and set the bottle on the table. "Have a Merry Christmas and all. I'll show myself out."

"Yeah, that's probably … No. Crap." Warren stopped him before Burt could walk back inside. "You're in no shape to drive. Gimme your keys."

Burt stared up at him. Finally, he shrugged. "Whatever." He fished his car keys out of his pocket. "Here you go."

With a quick apology to Beth, which included a cross-my-heart-double-icepick-death promise that Burt would never, ever, be allowed back inside the condo, Warren escorted his friend and all the geese to the elevator.

"Did you have to bring them with you?" Warren said as a Canada goose laid an egg in the middle of the corridor.

Burt snorted and pressed the **Close Door** button before all of the geese caught up with them. The doors closed, and like Christmas ghosts, the last two geese waddled through the otherwise solid doors. Only then did the elevator car move.

In the parking lot, Burt held out his hand. "Come think of it, you may want to let me drive."

"No, it's cool," Warren said. He unlocked the driver side door, and three Green Quaker Parrots and a Scarlet Macaw flew out in a flurry of feathers. Warren threw up his arms and staggered back. "Shit!"

"Told you," Burt said.

As the birds screeched and squawked overhead, Warren gaped in amazement. "What. The. Hell?"

"Calling birds." Burt moved around the car and took the keys dangling from Warren's limp fingers.

"I am never driving with you again," Warren said, prying his fingers off the dash.

Burt belched. "Heard that before."

"The birds, they kept ... and through the windows like ... Jesus!" Warren opened the passenger side door. An egg landed on the asphalt in a glistening smear and pieces of broken shell.

They'd parked at the far end of the apartment lot, away from the majority of the cars. Six Canada geese milled about, passing in and out of a battered blue Toyota Corolla, looking for tasty bits on the pavement.

Burt sagged against the car. Warren came around the back, surprised to find the space at Burt's feet free of eggs. Like smoke, a goose slipped out of the car and deposited one between Warren's feet. "What the hell is going on here?"

"I have a bird problem. Kind of a long story." Burt burped and headed towards the stairs, crushing the occasional egg with impunity on his way. "Okay, not really, but come on upstairs anyway."

Warren followed, rather helped, Burt to the second floor and headed to the apartment at the end of the walk. Burt paused, key at the lock, and looked at Warren. "You ready?"

Warren nodded, shook, bobbled his head. "No."

Burt snorted, and opened the door.

A potted pear tree stood in the middle of the entry, a tiny dun partridge nested in its leaves. Warren frowned. "Maybe you should ... Hey!"

Burt pushed the pot over with the toe of his boot and staggered by. The partridge hopped up and down the length of the trunk, huffing and clicking with breathless ire.

"Make yourself at home," Burt said. "Everything else has."

Warren carefully stepped over the fallen tree and into the apartment. "Wow. You really got it going on in here, don't you?"

"Y'think?"

A single table lamp illuminated kitschy Christmas decorations scattered around the apartment: a variety of nutcrackers; a tiny artificial tree in the center of the dining room table; a stuffed Santa Claus and three reindeer wedged into the cushions of the couch; a menorah sporting a red felt hat with white fur trim.

Two dun and gray birds cooed complacently on the top of a bookshelf covered with smears and pools of white. A pair of Maran hens strut and clucked under the coffee table. Warren thought he heard a third chicken somewhere, but could not find it. The geese, now three Canada geese, two Atlantic Brant, and one Lesser White-footed goose, meandered as they cared to, laying eggs every dozen steps or so. By the laundry nook sat two plastic clothes baskets filled with even more eggs. The place smelled of feathers, mustiness, and the throat-clogging stench of bird droppings.

Warren followed Burt into the kitchen, pointing back over his shoulder. "Those are turtle doves, aren't they?"

"Yup."

"Man, I thought they were just part of that Christmas carol, you know?"

"You get used to it. Wanna beer?"

"Um ... sure." Warren watched one of the Brant pass through the kitchen wall on its way to the bedroom. His left hand closed by reflex on a cold can, his right opened it, and he had it half gone by the time he thought to blink. "You weren't kidding when you said you had a bird problem."

"Nope." They wandered into the living room, where Burt knocked three eggs on the floor and made himself comfortable on the couch. He motioned to the easy chair piled with eggs. "Take a load off."

Warren compromised by perching on the arm of the chair. "So, is there something you want to tell me?"

"I'm cursed."

The third hen, a Faverolles, a happenstance knowledge of breed that continued to amaze Warren, came out from behind the TV stand and wandered down the hall. Warren watched it turn the corner into the bathroom. "No, seriously, I can take it."

"I am serious."

Warren stared at Burt. "Cursed."

Burt sighed and shook his head, then sank deeper into the cushions. "Do I look like the kind of guy to take up urban farming?"

Warren sipped his beer without tasting it. "No," he said after some thought, "but cursed is, that is, being cursed is ... "

"Pretty fucked up?"

Warren nodded. "Yeah."

Burt took a pull from his beer, wiped his mouth on his sleeve. "Do you remember Mala?"

"The blonde pixie cut?"

"That was Amanda."

Warren pursed his lips in thought, then nodded. "Mala. Yeah, yeah. Wasn't she the one with dark hair and some serious ... " He cupped a hand in front of his chest.

Burt nodded. "That's the one. She took off last week."

"That sucks, and right before Christmas, too. I was wondering why I hadn't seen her around." Warren peered over Burt's shoulder. "Hey, that goose just swallowed a bone. Shouldn't you ...?"

Parrots babbled and cawed from the kitchen. Burt stared at him.

Warren took another sip. "Yeah, right. Sorry. You were saying?"

The goose in question walked into Burt's chair an Atlantic Brant and out the other side a Snow Goose.

"Anyway, it got pretty ugly. She said things, I said things, she said I didn't respect her cultural needs, and she split. Then Saturday, she calls me saying she thinks I need to learn a lesson about generosity and thoughtfulness, maybe that will set me straight."

A Faverolles hen hopped onto Burt's chest; he pushed it off. The bird flapped a few feet and came to rest on the dining room table piled with pizza boxes and Chinese take-out containers.

"The next day, what to my wandering eyes should appear but a God damn partridge in a pear tree when I'm getting ready for work. Scared the bejeezus out of me when I came out of the shower. I nearly broke my fool neck."

Warren cringed. "Dude."

Burt finished his beer, crumpled the can, and threw it at the turtle doves on top of the bookcase. The birds flew twice around the room before displacing a Camelot Macaw on top of the bedroom door. "Tell me about it. I called in sick on Saturday because the damn thing kept following me around the house."

Warren's eyes widened. "Excuse me?"

Burt nodded, twisted around to look over both shoulders. "I don't see it. Probably in the bedroom."

The entry was empty. Warren moved carefully around the yolk stains on the carpet to the bedroom. The pear tree, complete with partridge and pot, stood at the foot of the bed. Much to the partridge's dismay, the Camelot Macaw had claimed part of the foliage for itself.

"You were right," Warren said.

"Thought so."

Warren made his way into the kitchen. "You want another beer?"

"Sure."

A Greylag Goose sat in an open utensil drawer. At Warren's approach, it jumped to the floor and waddled away, leaving an egg nestled amidst the spatulas and potholders. As if approaching a strange dog, Warren reached out and touched the egg. The shell felt warm and a bit sticky. He wiped his finger on his pants, and opened the refrigerator. He wrinkled his nose. "There's bird shit all over in here, man."

Burt snorted. "The fridge?"

"Yeah."

"Yeah, the chickens like to check things out in there sometimes."

Warren swallowed a cheap joke about Kentucky Fried Chicken and carried the beers back to the living room. "So, what are you going to do?"

Burt downed three swigs in short order. "I don't know, man, I really don't." He looked and sounded like a kicked dog. "I haven't been to work in nearly a week. Clarkeson called yesterday asking what was up. I told him I had a family emergency, but he's not gonna buy that forever."

"It's not that bad. I mean, it's not like they follow you everywhere." Warren paused. "Right?"

Burt sighed. "The tree and chickens tend to stick close to home, but you saw what happened with the others."

Warren put on his best buddy smile. "At least you have the rings. That's something."

Burt nodded. "Yeah, they're not so bad when they show up on my fingers or in my pockets. Not real gold, though." He finished his beer.

"Where do they ... Never mind."

Burt made a sound somewhere south of a laugh. An African Gray Parrot perched on the stereo mimicked the sound perfectly. Burt threw the empty can at the bird, and began to cry.

"Aw, c'mon, man, no." Warren got Burt some toilet paper, and they sat together until Burt's tears stopped and the hens had made off with the tissue. "Have you tried, maybe, calling Mala?"

"She won't answer. Hasn't returned my calls. Won't answer when I knock."

Warren did some figuring. On the off chance he was wrong, he checked the date on his phone. "Listen, hey, um ... do you know what day it is?"

Burt shook his head, wiped his nose on his sleeve.

"You're on the sixth day of this Christmas thing, right?" Warren said. "Well, technically all this is supposed to be for after Christmas, but whatever."

Burt nodded.

"And there are only twelve days of Christmas."

Another nod.

Warren checked his calendar a final time. "Today is the tenth, well, eleventh now. There are fourteen more days until Christmas, and only six more days of the song. What happens then?"

Burt rubbed his face with both hands. "No idea. I don't have that much room in my apartment."

Warren held up his phone. "Maybe I can call her for you."

From the bathroom came the splashing of water and the trumpeting of swans.

But Calm, White Calm, was Born into a Swan

The words of a half-remembered Christmas song became seven swans circling the sky in a halo of white. They took with them memories and thoughts, and left First Sergeant Keith Lamont, 1st Battalion, 12th Marines, sitting alone on the sand.

He wondered: "Why?"

"Because."

A lady in a dress of rainbow feathers stood at his side. She had wide blue eyes and a mouth a touch too small for her square chin. "Ready?"

She smiled and held out a hand.

Keith got to his feet and looked around. At the vague smears on the ground, dark greens and reds, blacks and browns. At the hulking shape to the east that smoked, and other, smaller, shapes dashing around it pointing sticks at one another. "I ... Where? I mean, I guess so."

He tried to remember why it was important that he remember what he'd forgotten, but he couldn't, so he took the lady's hand and together they went up.

First they passed through the white that blinded, and he could not see; then through the red that burned, and he screamed his soul charred. Finally, they passed through the blue that soothed, and he slept.

He woke on green grass beside a mirrored lake that reminded him of Minnesota, fishing with his uncles and grandfather. The air tasted sweet and not at all like sand or diesel fumes. Would he find Uncle Georgie's cabin if he followed the shoreline to the hills in the distance? The

Nickleback Cafe where they served French fries with a cup of brown gravy on the side?

Shadows passed overhead. Keith looked up to find seven swans flying high above, brilliant slashes of white against the blue. The birds circled seven times before dipping low and alighting in the lake. White became black and charcoal and light gray upon reflection in the water. The swans swam to the shore, and Kevin knew this was how it would be. No cut and dry answers, only reflections of considerations of opinions of acts of war.

Men. Young and old, clean shaven and bedraggled, sometimes in uniform, sometimes white feathers, waded out of the lake in front of him. Their clothes, like their feathers, were dry. Keith gave each his full attention: a lanky blonde in olive drab; two Asians wearing khaki; a black man dressed in a loose orange cotton tunic and baggy pants; a dark-haired Eurasian wearing a blue uniform coat with a fur collar; a crew-cut brunette with a scar that pulled the left corner of his mouth towards his eye. The last, a Middle Eastern man with wide brown eyes and a black-and-white checked keffiyeh, looked familiar in a way that settled hot and tight in Keith's gut.

"Hello!" the Middle Eastern man said. Keith heard English, but the man's lips moved in time with another language.

Keith stepped away from the feeling, uncertain why he could not face it. "Do I know you?"

The man smiled, showing a mouthful of tobacco-stained teeth. He clapped Keith on the back. "Yes, but not in the way you think."

Keith remembered quick shapes running around with sticks. Some were brown, and showed their teeth with angry screams. "Then how?"

The seven men smiled. "In time, brother," the shorter of the two Asians said. "Give yourself that much. Do you like music?"

The sun set and rose.

Keith couldn't recall how he passed the time, or if it passed at all. Had he slept? Eaten? He didn't feel tired, or particularly hungry. His sense of *now* blurred and ran like watercolor paints. Certain memories of before *now* drew blood when he tried to touch them, so he left them to blood and forgetfulness.

Keith sat with the men around a small fire ringed with stones where they told crass stories and jackass jokes, what chaplains and counselors called "coping mechanisms". The one about the Pole with an imaginary machine gun. The English lieutenant assigned to his new post in the desert. Or the time the Coolie was caught with his head up a sheep's ass. Keith listened; sometimes he smiled. Then frowned.

The men accepted his silence. The jokes gave no quarter, struck like bullets—*Cunt, Chinaman douche, Fat-assed dyke, Oil-slick sumbitch, I shoved my barrel so far up his fag ass.* Yet for every offensive word or intent there was a look, a gesture, that forgave both the teller and the offended. Sons of different mothers, the men were brothers under the skin. This, at least, Keith understood.

He looked beyond the men to the lake, unable to shake the feeling that the world forgot itself and faded whenever he looked away. He worried at the thought like he would a hole in his gums after having a tooth pulled, exploring the edges of something no longer there. He tried to smile around the emptiness, but could only manage the occasional nod before walking away as the swans followed the Eurasian man through another chorus of *Katyusha.*

Keith wandered the lakeshore, skipping rocks, making a whistle from a piece of grass the way he had as a boy. Small flocks of colorful birds kept him company in branches and the sky, sometimes flying low over the water as if admiring their reflection. On a lark, he took off his boots and socks, rolled up his uniform pants, and waded into the cool water.

Smooth stones massaged his feet, and tiny white fish darted under every step. In another place and time, he would have had a reflection. Here and now, he didn't. Keith couldn't say how he felt about that.

Sometime later, the lanky blonde swan found him and sat beside Keith on the low rise overlooking the lake. A long drink of water with hazel eyes and a three day growth of beard, the swan preened himself and sucked on a butterscotch hard candy. Together they watched rainbow birds dip and dive over the water.

"I have a wife and two kids," Keith said, when he found words that made sense. "Had. Marie, she's my wife. Julie, ten, and Brandon, seven. He'll be eight in June." He plucked a blade of grass, picked it to tiny green bits. "I usually carry a picture of them in my inside pocket, near my heart. I don't know what happened to it."

"Pictures and the like don't make the crossing," the swan said, sounding every inch from Liverpool. "Memories are the best way to be keeping things like that."

Keith nodded, accepting rather than understanding. "I guess." He held out a hand. "First Sergeant Keith Lamont, First Battalion, Twelfth Marines, Iraq."

The swan took Keith's hand in his own calloused grip. "Alec Tolliver, Corporal, Twenty-First Brigade, Eighteenth Battalion, half the bloody continent." He laughed. "For what it's worth."

They took turns skipping rocks over the lake, ripples advancing, mingling, retreating.

Keith scratched under his chin. "What happened?"

He wondered at the stillness of the words, how carefully he asked the question without touching the fears beneath it.

"To what?" said Tolliver.

"To me."

Whiz, skip, skip, skip, went the swan's rock. "You really want to know?"

"Yeah."

Tolliver hitched a shoulder. "A bomb under your truck."

"IED." Keith kept his gaze on the horizon. "Improvised explosive device."

"You said it." The swan hefted another stone. "Truck went flip and tumble, men started running and shooting."

Keith tongued the hole in his memory. He recalled the dry, sandy heat, the painfully blue sky, climbing into the truck. Nothing after that, until he heard the swans. "And ... I died?"

Tolliver nodded, gazing at him strong and steady, the stone unmoving in his hand. "You made it out of the truck, had helped three of your injured boys out and to shelter, when you caught a bullet with your face."

Keith rubbed the unmarred bridge of his nose. "I don't remember any of it."

"You may in time." *Whiz, skip, skip, skip.* Down went the rock.

Keith looked at his hands, slowly turning them over, his wedding ring on his left ring finger, a slender platinum band, his mother's wedding ring, on his right pinky. "So, you came for me because I died a hero?"

The swan shook his feathered head. "Not precisely."

Keith frowned. "Then why?"

Tolliver smiled. "What sets us Tommies apart is when a body and soul finds something worth fighting for, and end up dead for it. Comes time, though, there are them w'at think they have to stand-to instead of dying and needs a bit of prompting to move on. That's where we come in. We take fellas like you in for a time, let you rest a bit before going where ever you go."

"Oh." Keith looked at his hands again. "So, if I'm not ready to go, then, why am I dead?"

There. He said it, and a twinge of fear settled between his shoulder blades.

The swan smiled with an eyebrow and a corner of his mouth. "Because it happened, it's done, and now you move on. Ain't nofing wrong wif being dead, I'm supposing, but you're one of them that figures he can't die yet on account of needing to help no matter w'at the cost. This time the cost caught up to you."

"I never claimed to be some kind of Superman." The fear tightened to anger. "I never asked to die. I have plenty to live for."

The swan chuckled. "It's not me that needs convincing, Chumley."

Keith opened his mouth to protest and closed it again. He didn't want to be dead. His patrol needed him back in the fight. His family needed him. He needed, he wished ...

He wished for so many things, but wishes couldn't overcome the certainty in the swan's eyes.

A cyclone of tiny birds swept in over the lake. Keith looked for answers in their number, but they passed too quickly and were gone.

"I'm afraid," he said finally.

The swan nodded.

Keith picked up a rock and sent it tumbling into the lake without finesse. "What do I do now?"

"Rest," Tolliver said with a nod. "Life's hard, war's harder, so now you rest. Come a day, God willing, when there won't be no more war, but until then there's going to be those who don't want to let go just yet. Ones who understand we got to help each other, and that war isn't fought by prigs w'at take tea and biscuits between pulling the trigger." He laughed, a wry, tender trumpet call. "Well, not us enlisted, anyway."

Keith nodded, surprised at his own smile. "Yeah."

Tolliver stretched out, ankles crossed, hands behind his head, eyes closed.

Keith's thoughts chased themselves in circles until they collapsed from exhaustion. He twisted his wedding ring on his finger. "Marie complains, complained, sometimes that I've gotten a little rough around the edges over here. There. Iraq."

"And?"

"And I wonder what I would have been like if I made it home. Maybe it's for the best that I died. I can't, couldn't, can't ... fuck."

Keith pinched the bridge of his nose between his forefinger and thumb. He fought back a scream with the rhythm of breath before the first pull of the trigger. How sick was he to find that soothing? "I couldn't have gone home to the kids like this. I've done and said some pretty ugly things."

"Rougher than clicking another man?"

Keith frowned. "Clicking?"

The swan brought his hands up and mimed taking aim at Keith through a sight and pulling the trigger with the same ease of breath.

Keith closed his eyes against memories that called to him from behind the veil of blood and forgetfulness. "No."

"Then don't worry at it. No matter what them pansy arses at home say, all them funnies helped things make sense if only for a little while." Tolliver smiled. "Well, until the sand rat shot off your kisser, anyway."

Keith snorted. He picked up a rock. *Whiz, skip,*

skip, skip, skip. Better. "How did you die?"

"Threw a grenade out of the trench," the swan said in a low, calm voice, as if remarking on the weather. "Nowhere to run, so I did my best. Guess I didn't throw it far enough." He stared at the sun. "Suppose I could envy you, really. You died saving lives. I saved lives because I didn't want to die. Let me tell you, not easy to admit that. Took a right goodly amount of men and time to get to where I am now."

What could Keith say to that? Nothing, so he didn't try.

Tolliver eventually rolled up and got to his feet, brushing grass from his hands. "Come on. Let's get on back. They're having a swim."

"How do you ...?"

The swan honked.

Keith stood. "Right. Sorry."

They returned to find the brunette and the shorter Asian debating the virtues of soul music versus jazz while the other swans swam and splashed naked in the lake. Piles of clothes and gear lay in a glorious scatter at the water's edge.

Keith examined the haphazard array and realized there were no weapons amongst the gear.

As they approached, the men on shore nodded and those in the water called to the pair to join them. Keith glanced at Tolliver. "I wouldn't mind a swim. I mean, if it's allowed."

The blond swan looked over Keith's shoulder. "Not just yet."

Keith turned to find the woman dressed in rainbow feathers standing by a large rock near the shore. She looked at Keith, then turned her attention to the water. As one, the swans gathered round her with a ruffle of wings and shiver of tails.

All save Tolliver. The lone swan frowned. *"Oh?"* then his expression eased to a sudden awareness of joy and pain. "Oh."

At a loss, Keith looked from Tolliver to the woman. "What?"

The woman smiled at Keith. "Do you accept?"

Keith looked to Tolliver, now staring at him with an expression of longing, and home, and moving on. Keith felt hot sand against the remains of his face. He heard men yelling, the shriek of incoming artillery. His breath stilled in his chest. He only now realized what that meant.

Keith turned to the woman, thoughts of the men he'd lived and died for reflected in her eyes. "For how long?"

The other swans turned to him. The Middle Eastern man winked. One by one, they inclined their downy heads.

"That is for you to decide," a voice, his own, said in his mind.

Keith heard his wife's laughter, felt his children's arms around his neck. He needed rest. After that, time would tell. He bit his bottom lip until he could look at Tolliver without tears. The British Tommy stood at attention, eyes bright.

"At ease, soldier," Keith said. "You stand relieved."

Tolliver smiled, and disappeared in a hush of feathers on the wind.

Keith undressed. With his brothers, he stepped into the water and began to swim, a dark reflection gliding behind him.

A Milk of Human Kindness

"**M**ama?"

I kiss Amy Lynn's hair and hold her close. "It's okay, Bunny."

My little girl, my reason for everything that's happened, sticks her fingers in her mouth and snuggles against my chest. My nightdress is drenched with sweat. Outside the closet door, the seven ghosts move about, whispering my name.

"Dada?" Amy Lynn asks again.

"It's okay."

Four bony fingers slide under the door. Light pools like spilled milk around them.

"*Heather?*" a ghost whispers, shattered glass tearing through silk.

"Go away!" my fear says before I can stop it.

Amy Lynn gives a start and begins to cry.

Save for an icy patch at the bottom of the door, the closet is muggy and hot. Stifling. Heating ductwork and defunct plumbing runs up the back wall. I've wrapped spare bungee cords around the door knob, secured them to the pipe work, the rubber pulled tight to breaking like my last nerve.

I hunch in the farthest corner from the door, Amy Lynn on my lap, the red high heels Aaron gave me last Christmas pressed uncomfortably against my lower back. I didn't grab Aaron's cell phone, should have grabbed his cell phone. Not that the police can do anything.

"*We are so lonely, lonely, lonely.*"

Seven voices I once believed, that once sounded so sweet. I want to cover my ears to block out their insistent whispers, but to do that I would have to let go of my daughter.

"Dada?"

Aaron loves the house. Bay windows, wide staircase, walk-in pantry, claw-foot bathtub deep enough to completely submerge himself in steaming luxury and leave only his nose exposed to the world. Fixer upper on three acres, a mother-in-law house out back he can rework into his art studio. A dream come true ten miles outside Parkhurst city limits, away from the urban crush.

We pick out color schemes for each room. Aaron lays track lighting in the den. He and Amy Lynn bake a double chocolate, daddy-and-daughter "Welcome Home" cake. We make plans for a Christmas lights extravaganza.

Then come his headaches, the night terrors, the screaming. The doctor runs a full battery of tests, makes a referral to a neurologist. The verdict? Cluster headaches. For the dreams? Prazosin. Nothing works.

Summer greens fade to autumn's golds and browns. Aaron starts sleeping less, skulking around the house at odd hours. He's confused. Mutters to himself. Bit by bit, he pulls away. No more popcorn over late-night movies, fewer hours reading together in bed, no meals at the refinished dining room table. He spends hours in his studio, but never shares what he's working on the way he once did.

Two months ago, his art studio catches fire and burns to the ground. The conflagration fills the night with heat and acrid smoke. I scream *Help me!* and drag the hose behind me to spray the lawn and trees to keep the flames at bay.

Aaron stands on the back deck and watches his dreams burn.

The volunteer fire department blames faulty wiring,

but I can't shake the doubts after I find bits of copper wire in the pockets of Aaron's jeans. Aaron insists he had nothing to do with the fire, goes into a rage and starts throwing things when I press. I cling to the hope things will settle down.

"We can get counseling," I say one night after a particularly nasty, silly argument over kosher salt, of all things. "Please."

Aaron reluctantly agrees.

Pastor Warren recommends a qualified marriage counselor in Wellington. Aaron stops attending after the first session, announcing to God and the world that the counselor is an uptight cunt who can't diddle herself with both hands.

My husband never talks like that. He's changing, becoming someone I no longer know. I pray to God and the world that he will come to his senses.

He starts listening in on my phone conversations, following me into town, watching me sleep. My teetotaling husband begins to drink, beer and hard liquor, anything he can find some weeks. In an increasingly rare moment of honesty, when I ask him why, he says the drinking helps with the headaches. "And the dreams," he whispers, seated at the dining room table with a bottle of Captain Morgan's and a plastic coffee cup in front of him. "I just want to sleep, but the dreams ... "

My heart aches at the lonely-child fear in his voice. I want to wrap him in my arms and make everything better, but he wouldn't allow that even on a good day. I take a chance and put my hand on his arm. "Would you like to talk about it?"

He flinches and grabs his bottle. Hate stews at the bottom of his sleepless eyes. "What the fuck do you know?"

I sleep on the floor of Any Lynn's room that night.

And the day he finds me in the basement ...

Milk-white fingers curl around the bottom edge of the door. The wood turns gray, then white. It crumbles at the touch. The hand thrusts through the hole up to the wrist. *"We did as you asked,"* one of them says, hissing and screaming at once. *"We love you."*

From downstairs comes the splintering of heavy wood. I scream, Amy Lynn screams, and the ghost pulls another handful of splinters off the door.

I'm under the stairs looking for Christmas decorations when Aaron comes up behind me, blocking me in. "What are you doing?"

He stinks of beer and cigarettes. In the dim light of the single bulb all I can see of his face are his eyes, two bright spots in sunken sockets. I take a step back, Aaron a step forward. Fear burrows under my skin, makes me shiver. "Wrapping ... " I clear my throat. " ... Wrapping paper. I'm looking for wrapping paper."

He grunts, shakes his head, cocks it to one side. For a moment I think he's listening to someone, something, but I can't hear anything beyond my frantic heartbeat.

"Excuse me, please," I say, almost sounding calm. "I need ... need to get by."

He shakes his head again, a quick back and forth, a bull shaking off a fly. "No, no," he grunts. "No."

My thoughts go everywhere. Tumor? Drugs? Seizures? "Yes, please."

That's when he knocks the ribbon out of my hands and grabs me around the throat. "No."

He bends me back against the shelves, jerks my dress up, my panties down. No means *no*; he doesn't listen. I cross my legs, say the word we save for special occasions when things have gone too far. He slams the back of my head against the dry wall, and I see stars.

I scream with his first dry thrust. He covers my face with a moldy burlap sack. I struggle to keep quiet, more afraid for my life than my marriage.

Decay, rot, the reek of mold so thick I can barely breathe. The ghosts wail, beat against the walls, knock over furniture. One of them pushes her face against the hole. Thin lips pull back from blood black teeth. *"You promised,"* she sobs. *"We helped you and you promised. Promised!"*

"Get away!" I kick at her, knocking more wood away, widening the hole. "Fucking get away from me! Leave me alone!"

My mother suggests we fly down to Miami for the holidays. Does she suspect? I can't tell her, can't tell anyone. They would lock Aaron away. I still love him, and know I can help him. God help me help my husband find the man he used to be. That's all I want for Christmas, so I beg off with the twin excuses of work and weather. She's disappointed, but doesn't ask questions.

That's when my own dreams start, softly at first: the gentle hush of the stream at the back of the property. Naked women, light and dark, dancing under the trees, crying together, comforting one another with tender, knowing hands; those hands on my body, soothing Aaron's hate.

As the nights grow longer and Aaron confines me to the house, I confess to the women every hurt Aaron has ever done to me. In my dreams, I tell them, and I cry.

"Poor Heather. Let us help you," they whisper, coo, breathe against my skin. *"We can help you, keep you safe, teach him what it is like to hurt."*

For two weeks, I resist. Even in my dreams, I want things to get better, want my husband back, the man who brought me tulips on our third date and chocolate gelato on our honeymoon. The night he beats me and threatens Amy Lynn with a butcher's knife, I know it's over.

I'm a hostage to my daughter's safety. I can't leave Amy Lynn, it's too cold to risk taking her with me, can't call out, can't access the computer. Aaron paces downstairs like a caged beast, ranting at people who aren't there. I need to stay awake, but the weight of fatigue and fear push me into black sleep.

The women are waiting. They circle and soothe, stroke my hair, dry my tears. *"Poor, poor Heather."*

I can't take it anymore. Their kindness breaks me in ways Aaron's anger cannot. Yes, I say in my dreams. Yes, yes, yes! Don't let him hurt me ever again, don't let him near my daughter.

"We will help you, and then we can dance forever," say the women of my dreams. Seven women, seven voices, pale as milk in moonlight.

I wake to the sounds of I don't know what. Sucking, squeezing, slurping. Screaming. I hurry downstairs to find the seven bloody women decorating the Christmas tree with Aaron. His skin hangs from the tree in thin strips, his finger bones tucked amidst the boughs. A mass under the tree may be his body. I stand wide-eyed and frozen at the bottom of the stairs, too afraid to move. Then they come for me with blood slick open arms, and I run for Amy Lynn.

"We helped you, helped your daughter," the ghosts chant,

sing-song. "*You or daughter. You or daughter. Come for you or come for daughter.*"

I hold Amy Lynn tight, muffling the sounds of her cries against my night dress. "Hush, Bunny. Please."

The ghostly face pulls away, and with it another chunk of door. I can see the bloody feet shuffling on the other side.

Amy Lynn hiccups and smears her face against my chest. The Bungee cord holds the door closed, but won't prevent the ghosts from tearing through the wood. They'll kill us both. I believe in choices, in accepting consequences. God help me. I screw my eyes shut. "All right!"

Everything stops, the screams, the moans, everything but my daughter's tears.

Before I can think about it, I kiss Amy Lynn and push her off my lap. "No, Mama," she cries, grabbing my night dress, my hair. "No, no, Mama!"

I bury her in clothes torn off the hangers, wrapping them around her not so tight that she can't escape but tight enough that it won't be instantaneous. "I love you, Bunny. Mommy loves you. Never forget that."

"Mumu, Mumu," comes her voice from the writhing mass. "No, no, Mumu … "

I get to my feet, unwrap the cords, and throw open the door. The seven ghosts stand in a semi-circle, eyes intent on my face. "Don't hurt her," I manage to say without crying.

The center ghost nods once. Is she different from the others? Taller? Brighter?

"Please don't hurt her," I whimper.

She nods again, holds out bloody hands.

As my little girl screams and cries for me, I walk out of the closet and into the ghost's arms.

The first touch burns, the second chokes, and the

third snaps every bone in my body. With every bite and dredge, they introduce themselves.

The first, a young bride beaten to death on her honeymoon by her drunk husband when he can't perform. The farm is eventually bought at auction by a second couple. Desperate for comfort in the long, cold night of the dead, the maid encourages the husband to strangle his wife when she refuses to let him bring another woman into their bed. The third is that woman, and the first time they kill the man. And on, and on, to me, the eighth. They want women to comfort and keep warm. They come in dreams, to drive men mad and love women to death.

As they gorge on my blood and suck the marrow from my bones, I scream, then sob, then sigh with desire, and know them. Oh, my sisters, how I know them sweetly. They/We are lonely. They/We are hungry for love and life.

I am the eighth maid of the house, no longer a matron, no men for me. Cry, child, cry. Soon there will be a new family, a new man to hate and sister to love. Soon.

My skin falls at my feet, and I reach for my beautiful, beautiful sisters.

Oh, How She Danced

O nce there was a girl who destroyed a world, but first she danced.

Cho-Bet rode her bike to the top of the hill and stopped, shielding her eyes against the glare of the swollen red sun. Finding what she wanted, she climbed back on the rickety two-wheeler and continued riding.

An hour later, she stopped in the middle of the road and slowly climbed off the bike. Sensing her body heat, tiny puffballs popped, covering her feet and the remnant of paving stones in a cloud spores. Cho-Bet ignored the ankle-high purple clouds and pulled out Kemb-Kim's map. She adjusted her breather and spread the pliant bark over the bicycle seat, considering options and views.

Mushrooms the size of old-timey dream-shacks grew in clumps and rings along both sides of the road. To her left, mini-myconid-men, the tiny ThreeMs, not the larger, more self-aware TwoMs, shambled about, carrying wads of spore infested detritus from one pile to the next. This was a lonely time place, not at all what she expected.

Cho-Bet would have liked to look for someplace else, but Kemb-Kim's map showed a lady holding a stick above her head, and to her left was the remains of a statue of a lady holding a stick above her head, so this was the place. She walked the bike off the road to the right, carefully stepping around the largest patches of trilling ochre fuzz to reach a comparatively clear area behind a stand of bamboo 'shrooms.

Cho-Bet unloaded her knapsack, propped her bike against one of the stems, and built a fire from dried burn-shrooms and Kemb-Kim's map. Would have been nice to have Kemb-Kim around, to talksies with or maybe feelsies, but Kemb-Kim had turned back at the Big River Gorge. "You go on ahead," she'd said to Cho-Bet, smiling sad-like as she leaned on her staff.

Cho-Bet had opened her mouth to protest, but Kemb-Kim stoppered her with a wave of her hand and a shake of the head.

"It was all I could do to make it this far, Birdie," she'd said. Kemb-Kim was the only one who called her Birdie. Cho-Bet never knew why. "I can't go no fartherer." Then she'd pulled a worn leather-skin pouch out of her robes and presented it to Cho-Bet. "For you."

"I can't take the map. That's what you're for." Cho-Bet's voice had sounded brittle and small through the breather speak hole.

Kemb-Kim looked her right in the eye. "Haven't you been listen-earing? I'm not going no fartherer." She held out the bag.

Cho-Bet hesitated, then took the bag with a hating, and a longing, and a sadding. "Where will you go?"

Kemb-Kim shrugged. Her smile crinkled the edges of the gray fungal fuzz on her left cheek and wide chin. Without the fuzz, she looked just like Cho-Bet; with it, she looked goner. "Back to the lab-jamboree if I can." Kemb-Kim wiggled her bare toes in the dusty soil; tiny hairs along the tops and edges wiggled even more. "These mycelials want to put down every time I stop to catch my breath, and don't want me to starters when I got to move again. No place else to go but back to the start and take root." She tapped the bag, bringing up tufts of spores. "That is, no place that isn't come the end program of the world, anyway."

Cho-Bet felt weak in the knees, and wet salt stung her eyes. "But you did the final figurering. You is the alphamega."

"Silly Birdie. I just finaled what the hold-outs already figurered."

That's when Kemb-Kim tipped up Cho-Bet's breather and kissed her on the mouth, slipping a bit of meat between Cho-Bet's lips. Cho-Bet chewed without thinking—meat was meat, was meat, when there was no other food—and the bit of Kemb-Kim's tongue unraveled and filled her insides up to the top of her head with knowings.

Cho-Bet made wet salt noises. All the things she didn't want to know made her brain itch, her nose snotty, and clogged the ducts of her breather. "I don't want to be the alphamega," she said, burying her head in the crook of Kemb-Kim's neck. "I don't want to be aloner."

The other girl had hugged her harder, harderer even, and finally pulled away, holding Cho-bet by the shoulders. "There was niners, then eights, then seventies, and then all the way down to me, and now down to you. You're the alphamega now. End program."

And she turned and walked away, leaving the new alphamega to wonder what she'd done that was so horrible as to deserve the honor of end program for the world.

The memories came and went and turned to burn-shroom ash along with almost everythinger else: the knapsack; the extra shirt; the picking tools; Cho-Bet's breather. The first breath without the breather burned like shroom fire all the way down, but after coughing and spitting-up she began to feel better. The spores didn't waste any time. They settled into her blood; they turned the red sky even more red, made the soles of her feet itch and filled her mouth with cotton. Cho-Bet knew that she'd eventually take root or die, but if she died withouter dancing then the world wouldn't end and the eight holdouts beforer her would have carried the weight

of that possibility in vain. Being the alpha-mega, she knew this, and knowing, settled down beside the fire to get what sleep she could.

Cho-Bet scooted on her side away from the blue bush shroom. Once out of reach, she cut through the woody vine wrapped tightly around her calf. As she peeled the fibrous strand away, she hissed in pain, wet salt seeping out of her eyes. She rubbed at the growing welt, flicking tangles of fibrous mycelials from under her skin. Stupider hungry shrooms. Why couldn't they eat dead dirt things like everything else?

She cut back the ragged edges of her pants, then returned her knife to its sheath. In that short amount of time, her own pale pink mycelials had sprouted around the edges of the welt and now lay across the wound in a thin layer of skin. And they itched, oh, how they itched. Burned. Peppery fire hot, pee on open wound, chewing lemoners with a raw tongue burned. Cho-Bet gnawed on her palms until the welt healed over, the itching eased, and the urge to slice her own skin off in thin strips passed.

She leaned back on her hands and surveyed the low valley. 3Ms wandered in obscure patterns around her, TwoMs walkering counterpoint. Every now and then a TwoM extruded a wad of shroom stuff from the middle of its body stem and handed off the mass to a ThreeM who continued its walk about until it found a clear space and set its burden on the ground. Then it was back to walkering.

Her camp behind the bamboo shrooms was fine for sleeping, but wouldn't do for dancing. Too many rocks and puffballs, too many woody mycelials to trip a headspace focused on end programming the world. The red sun hung ready to drop out of the sky; she still had timer left before night to find a good dance place. The valley might do the trick.

She stood and brushed her hands on her pants, walkering into the throngs of ThreeMs, scratching absently where her shirt brushed the mycelials along her sides. Now and again her chest tightened and she stopped to catch her breath, wishering she hadn't burned her breather yester-before, wishering lots of things that didn't make any difference now.

Eventually Cho-Bet wandered down a gentle incline where shrooms that didn't like the cold-times rested dormant. She stopped in a low spot, a bowl inside a bowl, flexed her knees, kicked up dirt. Aside from a few TwoM stomachy bundles, this looked to be a good place, flat ground, big enough for a proper dance. She began tossing the surprisingly light bundles to the edges of the dip. No sooner had she grabbed the third bundle than a ThreeM returned the first two to their previous locations.

Cho-Bet scowled. "Hey! Step it back. I'm world-ending here."

She continued tossing shroom stuff away, and the ThreeM continued to bring it back. "I said stop," Cho-Bet said, kicking at the squat ThreeMs.

The little myconid man stepped out of the way. Cho-Bet over balanced and fell. She stood. The ThreeM retrieved a displaced bundle, bent to set the mass back where it belonged, and Cho-Bet slapped the ball out of the its hand. Her fingers scraping over the ThreeM's spongy flesh. "Get out of here!"

The ThreeM stepped back. Around them, the other myconid men stopped in their tracks and turned blank faces to Cho-Bet, not faces, really, folds in the fleshy annulus rings just under their caps. Each glowed and strobed iridescent rainbows over its gills and florescent spots.

Cho-Bet eased her knife out of the sheath, an eye out for a clear path if she had to run. The myconid men watched her and strobed. "I mean it," she said after a tenful of breaths. Kemb-Kim taught her to count to tenful so her brain could catch up before she went and did something stupider. "Clear on out."

Three breaths later, the myconid men turned as one and walked up slope until she could no longer see them.

Cho-Bet nodded, re-sheathed the knife. "That's better." She began to clear a proper dance ring.

The one thing that did not burn with everythinger else was the metronomer. Cho-Bet sat cross-legged by the low fire in the center of the dance ground and fished in her pockets for the remaining piece of the turning key, the key to the end program of the world. The tiny piece of metal rattled in her hand when she pulled it out, then dropped and lost itself in the dusty soil. "Ratterdamn," she swore under her breath, and spent whole minutes sifting through the dirt with both hands.

When she looked up, piece in hand, two ThreeMs stood on the far side of the fire.

Cho-Bet set the metronomer in her lap, covered it with one hand. "What do you want?" she said warily.

The little myconid men strobed and glowed.

"I don't talk 'shroom talk, so go on and go back to whateverer you were doing so long as it isn't cluttering up my dance place."

The ThreeMs did not move.

Cho-Bet sighed. "Finer."

She put them out of her mind, and turned her attention to fitting the bit of turning key into the back of the metronomer the way she'd seen Kemb-Kim practice every night since they left the lab-jamboree. Thoughts of her twosies made Cho-Bet's eyes give wet salt; she smeared it on her shoulders and focused on her hands. After a bit of fussing, she wedged the piece into place and began to carefully winder the metronomer, holding it so the turning key remained intact. With the final turn, Cho-Bet pressed a finger to the side of the key to keep it still. The metronomer thrummed in her hands, aliver. She looked up to find the ThreeMs watching her. "You still here?"

Strobe and flash, a ripple of blue dots.

"I don't got nothing for food any more. I won't be eating anything, and I know you don't eat livinger folks like me. You here to kill me because-because?"

Not a sound, save her breathing, and the wind spinning spores and dirt into tiny tornadoes.

"I'm going to dance now, so you better move out." Cho-bet stood, metronomer in hand. "I mean it. There's going to be fire, and lightning, and thunder-rain all over the place. I mean it. Go tell the others so you can get inside someplace. Anyplace. Go on."

The ThreeMs remained still.

"You're weird," she said, and meant each of the four sounds of the word.

Which didn't mean she wouldn't dance. Cho-Bet drew in a lungful of spores for inspiration, a way to remind herself that she had to dance no matter how the fear flapped in her stomach. She wanted to throw the metronomer away and run back to the lab-jamboree, turn back the clock with her runnings and make everything betterer again. But no, no, that couldn't happen. The world was tired and over, all done. She was the alphamega of the last holdout, and that meant it was up to her. Best this way, even betterer. Dance on her terms with no one to follow.

Cho-Bet set the metronomer in the dirt. The tiny box of wood with the metal swinging bar *ticked-tocked*, and end programmed.

Rust and spore take the ThreeMs. Cho-Bet slid her sinister foot into position for the first step of the alphamega dance, her dance now, then her dexter foot for the second step. Always best to start with the sinister foot because beginnings and endings were made up of darkness before anything else. Comfortable, brooding, nurturing dark, not the giant red sun that burned up the sky and grew closer every day.

Third step. Fourth.

She danced with knowings that went way back.

To Kemb-Kim. Webs-Di. Upt-Brid. To all the on-backs until the niner Jare-Mich, the firster holdout of them all who built the lab-jamboree. Jare-Mich had knowings from other folks who made the myconid men and fought the long ago trouble-times, but those knowings were too cluttered and spun up for Cho-Bet to dance like her own, something about twisting one helixes into two helixes and runna-knots, but even they helped lead Cho-Bet's feet. This dancing would finish the pattern and end everything, a key for the big compost-uterer. The stick lady would poke the sun, and all the sun stuff would spill out so there would be dark again. The end of the world. End program.

Cho-Bet breathed deep, tilted her face to the sky, eyes closed. The red sun stared at Cho-Bet through her eyeskins. On her first pass of the ThreeMs, her hand brushed against their caps. Cho-Bet brought her hand up to her face, opened her eyes. Her fingers glowed miniature rainbows.

Cho-Bet danced. She removed her shirt and then her pants, tossing them into the fire. The ThreeMs did nothing when she took off her first shoe, but when she pulled off her second shoe and threw that into the fire they feller in step behind her and began to dance along.

What do you think you're doing? she wanted to say. Go on, get out of here. But she'd started the dance and it ran thick in her. She didn't have the knowings to speak anymorer. She could feel the dance working on her body, mixing with Kemb-Kim's knowings to end everything. So, let them dance along. Couldn't be too bad, seeing that they were as much girl folk as she, making sprouts and other ThreeMs. Laydemis, Jare-Mich would have called them. No, wrong word. Layeedems. No. Neverer mind.

Faster she danced, tiny cilia extruding from her pores. She tasted red, saw the sounds of her feet on the soil, smelled the air pressure as more ThreeMs entered the circle. First oner, then twosies, finally sixties, and seventies total. A TwoM joined them, its cap a bouncing blur, together with Cho-Bet making niners in all. The myconids waved their stumpy arms and thick fingers, stomped their stemmy feet in time with the metronomer. Niners layeedems danced around the fire.

Cho-bet's feet slid in the soil until her skin peeled away. New cilia formed and then broke off the next turn around. Gills fluted and disintegrated. She laughed hard and long, giddyish with the pattern unwinding. Faster now, her skin shed itself. Fingernails dropped to the soil and scuttled away. Hair flew off her head. Her eyeballs dissolved; she sucked them into her lungs to watch from within. Faster, Cho-Bet, faster, faster. Dance, Cho-Bet, faster, faster. Dance.

The wind joined the dance, stealing strands of Cho-Bet, depositing them on the myconid men. The strands coaxed their way inside the myconid. *Hello, Layeedem Cho-Bet. Join us at the end of the world, join us and make it new again.*

Voices? From where? New again? No, no. End program.

Yes. Dance, alphamega, be the end all and beginning all. If then, goto, untwist, reravel.

Cho-Bet laughed to the sky and the dance. Her tongue swallowed itself, and was stolen away.

And when she danced herself away, the myconid-men, small and large, left the fire, went back to their piles, taking the omega and the alpha with them.

Once there was a girl who remade the world, but first she danced.

Git Along Little Dogies

The man in tights, bells, and a doublet of crushed burgundy velvet stood with chin up and arms extended. "Harken to me, good fellows! Where might I find ... "

Pico Dentale jerked his thumb over his shoulder. "That way. Follow the laughter."

The man bowed low. "My thanks!" he said, and bounded over the chuck wagon into the darkness.

The thirteen men around the cook fire listened to the offended *vacas* shuffle and complain, and the heady *Huzzahs!* when the stranger found the others.

"That's ... what ... seven? Eight so far?" Carl said finally.

Pico threw the dregs of his coffee into the fire. It hissed and made the night smell a little less like *vaca* shit. "Nine," he said, setting his cup beside him on the ground.

Stan snorted on Pico's left. "Said you should have run the first two off."

Pico cut a piece of tobacco off the twist and tucked it between his cheek and gum. The tangy wad burned a moment, then his spit began to flow and turn the fire to juice. He didn't much feel like dealing with the older man, but he shrugged with good humor and said, "I get paid to be a trail boss and drive cattle. Can't no one pay me enough to draw on a man without him having a go at me first, *amigo*, not even men like those *hombres*, whatever they are."

He patted the Colt on his hip, drawn twice in the past two years to shoot at coyotes. The other men sniggered and guffawed. Pico hid his smile by wiping a hand across his mouth.

Stan cut him an ornery look and spit chaw juice off

to the side without landing too near to Pico's feet. "So long as they don't get so bad as them geese near Denver a few years back."

That earned a full round of laughter.

Pete poked Cookie in the shoulder. "Geese. You remember that, huh, Cookie? The geese, they … "

And the two drew the rest of the men into the story of geese, and eggs, and feathers in embarrassing places. Pico listened for a time before excusing himself to head for the bushes, both because he was tired of tussling with Stan, and because he genuinely had to piss.

Dried grasses and loose rocks crunched underfoot with every heavy step after hours in the saddle. The rustling of the *vacas* and the skitterings of small things in the grass filled the silence beneath the laughter of his crew and the cheers of the jumping *hombres* in funny clothes. The chill Texas night rattled up his spine and across his shoulders, not that Pico minded. He'd had enough of heat riding the herd.

Away from the press of bodies, he searched the sky for familiar shapes in the stars, a habit from boyhood. There was *Oso Menor*, and *Oso Mayor*, and to the east *Tauro*. There were many, many more, but Pico couldn't recall the names his *abuela* sang on her front porch of a night much like tonight, when the saints drew close and waited for *Jesucristo* to be born.

How many days until *Navidad*? Three? Probably. He was too tired to remember the day of the week, let alone his advent calendar. With any luck, he could celebrate *Navidad* with a bath in a real tub, maybe a meal that didn't have to be soaked, or cured and cut with coffee. His stomach rumbled in anticipation at the thought.

He would have liked to spend the holiday with friends and family, but driving cattle from San Antonio to Kansas City or Dodge City wasn't a bad way to live.

As the trail boss, he ran men, checked brands, and kept an eye out for trouble. Sometimes he spent a night or two in town with a woman who had most all of her teeth. He had five ounces of gold in the bank box back in San Antonio, and might have another two by the end of next year if he managed his pay.

Of course, he wouldn't always be a trail boss. Someday he'd buy into his brother-in-law's property, maybe with a wife and a few hundred head of cattle. The *gringos* in their fancy houses might not like it, but folks back in San Antonio would know his name and that made all the difference.

Yup, it was a good life, though on nights like this, with only a few *hombres* and *vacas* for company, Pico sometimes stared at the sky and wished, if only for a moment, that he was a boy again sitting with his *abuela* on a small wooden porch, smelling the smoke of her clay pipe and listening to her sing.

Pico yawned. No doubt about it, when thoughts like that came around it meant he was plumb worn down.

He was buttoning up his pants when a dark-skinned man in gold and white pantaloons and a crown of gold stars landed with a curt bow on the other side of the bushes. *"Hola!"*

Pico accidentally caught a couple of hairs in a button hole. He jumped and swore and bit his bottom lip to keep from screaming.

The man struck a pose, hands on his hips, one foot tipped just so. "Can you direct me to a gathering of such nimble men as I who find solace and purpose in the making of merriments?"

Pico waved over his shoulder, beyond the chuck wagon and fire. "That way," he said between clenched teeth.

"Gracias." The man flexed his knees, and leapt away.

Pico waited until his eyes stopped watering before he turned back to the fire. At the north end of the two-thousand head herd, the *vacas* complained long and low, the sound rippling back towards camp with the shuffling of hooves and sharp whip of tails against flanks. Above that came the whooping and hollering of men leaping back and forth, clapping and cheering one another on.

Pico stopped by Cookie, who was sorting through a

bowl of dry beans. "You take good care with those Pecos strawberries, Cookie."

The trail cook *hrumphed* deep in his chest. "I'll do what I want with them, that's all you gotta know." He tossed a small rock into the dark.

A colorful shout from the dancing men startled the cattle and had the *vaqueros* peering into the night. Cookie didn't look up from the beans. "Better get something done about that before them cows get to thinking about running."

Pico stifled a yawn, nodded. Fatigue had ridden hard over common sense, and it was high time he sent those men on their way. "*Sí.*"

He stepped over to the fire. "Listen up."

The men settled and turned to him, firelight tucking shadows in the creases of their faces.

"Stan, take Pete out and tell them men they got to be going now. Miles, Lee, and Charlie, you get a couple of horses and start riding the line. Turn the leads right if they look to start running."

Stan set his coffee cup down, and stood. "Bout time." He spit at Pico's feet.

Pico grit his teeth, wishing Stan were a coyote on four legs and not two. He crossed his arms over his chest. "You can always stay at the fire. Suit yourself, *amigo.*"

The men got moving, even Stan. Most regarded Pico as good and fair, but all agreed you didn't cross the man who gave out the pay at the end of the drive.

Pico had taken off his hat and washed his face, thinking about tomorrow's hard ride, when he heard the sharp crack of gunfire and a tumble of panicked screams. He rushed towards the north end of the herd. "Cookie, shut her down! Wilbur, get to the horses!"

He struggled past the *vacas* surging against one another to get away from the sound, and hurried with the rest of the men into the night.

A figure soared overhead in the moonlight, and then another. Screams turned to a cacophony of laughter and angry shouts. A third figure leapt high above Pico and landed on the back of a longhorn a bare arm's length away. The *vaca* tried to turn and bolt, but just as fast the man in yellows and greens leapt off its back and was gone again.

"I said stop all that bouncing or I'm gonna bounce you right on your ass!"

That was Stan, and he *did not* sound happy.

A voice Pico didn't recognize, cultured and decidedly English: "But, sirrah! We were only ... "

Pico shouldered a *vaca* to the side and stormed into the clearing of packed dirt and trampled grass. He slowed to a ponderous walk as he came to the crowd. "You were only *what?*"

The near full moon shone bright enough that Pico made out Stan and Pete, and the ten fancy-dressed men. He set his fists on his hips. "What the hell is going on here?"

The ten men laughed and leapt into the air, turning somersaults and triple twists as they went.

"That's what's going on," Stan said like an angry wolf, jabbing his free hand in their direction. His other hand gripped his own Colt tight, but he had sense enough to keep the gun at his side. "They got their feather heads up their Mary asses and they is going to get themselves killed if they ... I said to put an end to that!"

This last was directed to a pair of men turning back flips over one another. Maybe out of reflex, Stan raised his pistol. Pico pushed the man's hand down. He strode over to the frolicking pair. "You got a problem listening to the man? Sounded to me like he spoke clear enough."

Stan stood head and shoulders taller.

The two men looked at one another, and then at Pico. Something of his authority must have conveyed itself, for the one in peach silk said, "We have too much joy not to express it by leaps and bounds."

"That's all well and good, but enough is enough." Pico turned a slow circle, looking every *vaquero* and fancy man in the eye until they kept still and he knew for certain he had their undivided attention. "Now, you listen to me. And you WILL listen."

A handful of *vacas* shied away at the hot edge to his voice. Pico trusted his men would keep things from getting out of hand, and if that didn't work, well, he'd think of something later. One crisis at a time.

Pico continued, "I was plenty nice when the first of you showed up, but now it's time for you to be on your way."

A blonde fellow in a green leather jerkin and brown pantaloons—Pico recognized him as the fifth to arrive—stepped forward. "Truly we appreciate your efforts to maintain order, but the blessed day of Christmas approaches and we ... "

Pico glared down at the small, fragile looking fellow. "Are you gonna do what I say, or I am gonna show you how we make men jump in Texas, and what we do with those who jump too slow?" He drew his gun and cocked the hammer.

The man took a step back. "Here now. We leap and cavort to express our gratitude to the world. There's no reason for any of this."

The other fancy men murmured in agreement.

"Glad to hear it, but go do your *expressioning* someplace else." Pico spit chaw juice at the man's feet. "I don't know where you folks come from, or where you head to when you leave, but I figure you're ready to head on." Again he turned a slow circle. "Now."

Pico didn't care to shoot, but so help him God he'd put a hole in any one of these leaping fools if they made him look bad in front of his men.

The ten men looked at one another. Stan and the other *vaqueros* stood a little straighter. Pico slid his finger over the trigger.

The man in white and gold stepped forward. "*Sí*," he said, and bowed from the waist.

One at a time, the ten men bowed much the same until all had agreed, and as one they bent their knees and leapt into the air. Up, up they went, and did not come down, disappearing into the night sky.

Only the *vacas* had anything to say about it, and not for long before they settled.

Pico took a deep breath. He holstered the Colt. "Let's get these cows settled down," Pico said with clipped, precise authority. "Got a lot of miles tomorrow, and it's getting late."

Stan nodded at the others, and spit his chaw juice away from Pico. "You heard the man. Round 'em up."

Pico set Pete and Wilbur to watch the *vacas* for the rest of the night. A petty little voice inside insisted he put Stan on watch for firing the first shot, but Pico figured he'd settled into a truce with the older *vaquero*. Best to call it *Feliz Navidad* and leave it at that.

Pico had settled down by the fire with a last sip of water and a bit of jerky when he heard birdsong, the silver rippling of water, the running of feet and laughter. The sounds wrapped themselves around a cascade of notes that dipped and soared and then stilled as a man dressed in silvers and greens stepped out of the fire. He carried a wooden flute.

"Greetings," he said with a bow and tip of the cap.

"I am a piper sent to play for ten lords-a-leaping. Where might they be found?"

Re: Pete

A knock on the workshop door.

Pete groaned. "Come in."

The door opened, and Paris and Piper stepped inside.

"Honey, Piper has something to show you," Paris said, all sparkles, and dangling icicle earrings, and You-will-show-some-holiday-cheer-or-I-will-go-all-Krampus-on-your-ass behind her smile.

Pete twisted his face into his best Give-me-a-break-I'm-trying-to-figure-things-out-here grin. "Sure. What'cha got for me, sweetie?"

Piper bounced over to her father and presented him with a picture of a dog sitting in a field of blue and pink flowers.

"For you!"

Pete took the picture, searching for something, anything, honestly appreciative to say. "Honey, that's great. You ... you even managed to stay inside the lines this time." He set the picture on the desk behind him on top of the other pictures, next to the coffee mug with eggnog and an extra four fingers of spiced rum.

"I love you, Daddy," his daughter said, and she hugged him as hard as she could.

Pete managed to return the hug without cringing overmuch. He looked over Piper's bright red braids to his wife's You'd-better-figure-it-out-pronto-Mister-I-Can-Fix-It glare. "I love you, too, honey. Why don't you, um, head into the game room? You're Xmasakah present is waiting for you."

Piper's blue eyes widened. "Really deally?"

He couldn't help it. Pete's smile softened at her expression, at everything about her. At least for a moment.

"Really deally."

"Oh, thankyouthankyouthankyouthankyou!" Piper squealed, and hugged him again until he couldn't breathe.

"Okay, Piper, let's go see your Xmasakah present," Paris said, and took the girl by the hand. "Let's leave Daddy to his work, okay?"

Piper bounced to the door. "Okay!"

"Hey, sweetie?" Pete said before the door closed. "How many fingers am I holding up?"

Piper looked over her shoulder. "Oh, Daddy! Always bamfunning!"

"Yeah, hehe, that's me," Pete said. "Always ... always bamfunning."

Piper tugged on her mother's hand. "Moooom, come ooooon!"

Paris blew him a I-mean-it kiss, and closed the door with an ominous, loving click.

Leaving Pete with the eggnog and a Xmasakah problem the likes of which God had never seen.

He grabbed the most recent picture and examined it in detail, searching for the minutest hint of a difference. Nothing. Without a doubt, this was one of Pipers pictures, well, not Piper exactly. Piper number seven. Eight? Pete rifled through the other pictures in the stack, six total. Piper Seven. He would have to start tattooing numbers on their foreheads. Oh, please, please, don't let it come to that point.

From down the hall and two rooms over he heard his daughter: "Piper!"

And his daughters piped in: "Piper!"

Pete finished the eggnog in three gulps and dropped his head on his desk. "Oh God."

Six years ago, the news that Paris could not conceive nearly crushed their dreams of a bio-family, but modern wonders and a sufficient credit balance gave them the daughter they'd always wanted.

They'd contracted for Piper's conception, selected her hair and eye color, her love of cats and cooking, her eventual acceptance into Harvard to study particle physics, and eagerly waited for her implantation in a certified womb specialist. Paris spent the entire gestation picking out a layette and matching security perimeter. She even dyed her eyes a fetching pink to match the wallpaper.

Ten months to the day after implantation, Pete and Paris attended the delivery of beautiful, slimy, squalling Piper with wisps of bright red hair plastered to her head. Their daughter grew, cooed, and pooed. Adoring, funny, insightful, Piper loved everyone and everyone loved her in return. Her declaration the morning of her first natal celebration: "Mama, I want to hug the world."

Her gift to them on her sixth natal celebration five weeks ago: "I want a baby sister."

Well. Not the hand woven hemp basket they expected, but certainly easier to manage than her first gift so many years before. Snuggled together later that night, Pete and Paris talked about the possibilities. Certainly they had enough love in their hearts and rooms in their house for another genetically hand-crafted bundle of joy.

Pete contacted the conception agency only to learn that they had closed their doors months ago. Something about pretty men and embezzling samples. So the family browsed the catalogues and finally made an application with another agency, less prestigious, yes, but still favorably recommended by friends and womb donors alike.

Of course, they weren't the only family thinking

of expanding, and that meant a twenty-three month waiting list. Piper collapsed in tears after the application interview. "But Daaaaddy," she said. "I want a baby sister!"

Pete had gathered his daughter in his arms and showered her with kisses. The love in his daughter's heart wouldn't bring her any closer to a new sister.

"Don't worry, hon," he'd said, securing her eighteen point harness in the backseat. "You'll get your baby sister."

Pete knew what he had to do, if not how.

Later that night, after two bottles of wine and a satisfyingly sweaty snuggle, Pete came up with an idea and Paris agreed. They would make Piper a baby sister themselves. All it took was ingenuity, some specialized equipment, and a sample of Piper's genetic material from her tooth swabs. Paris was so enthused by the thought that she bought a case of wine and cleared Pete's schedule for the next week.

Pete got hold of a friend of a friend, who knew someone who had a certified friend who helped him find the best deal on replicator equipment and an experimental uterine accelerator. Good-bye spring vacation, hello second-mortgage bomb. Pete set to work. To supplement his own tactical genetics engineering degree, he bought the chips and scripts from a genetics major taking a sabbatical to Maui, and spent the next four months hip deep in DNA kits and coffee. Paris gave him frequent foot massages. Piper wrote letters to her new sister, hoping they would like many of the same things.

A sharp knock at the door. Pete finished pouring another finger of rum, and screwed on the cap with care. He looked at the clock. It couldn't be that late; he still had rum left. "Yo."

Piper burst through the door, a pink feather boa

wrapped around her neck. "Look, Daddy! Look what I found!"

The boa purred and rubbed the top of its head under Piper's chin.

Paris stepped in behind her, a few gray hairs here, missing a few more hairs there. "She found it at the back of the garage near the accelerator, didn't you, sweetie? Its name is Pickles."

Piper rolled her eyes. "Mooooom, it's Sweet Pickles."

Paris shrugged. "Sorry. Sweet Pickles."

Well? said Paris' eyebrow.

Pete gave a Allahsus-I'm-doing-my-best eye roll. "That's great, honey. Really deally. Yeah."

"Mama's going to take me to meet my new sister," this Piper, said. "She says my sister will love Sweet Pickles."

Paris held up eight fingers, eight I-am-not-a-happy-woman fingers, ticking them off one at a time. "It will be great, honey. Let's leave Daddy to work, hmmm?"

"'kay!" Piper ran up to Pete and threw her arms around him. The boa hissed and squirmed between them. "I love you, Daddy. Thank you soooo much."

And they were gone.

Pete sipped his rum. "Maybe there will be three ghosts, and I'll wake up and it will be Xmasakah all over again."

He checked the time, and sighed. Best to get back to work just in case.

He returned to the plans and circuits, the entire genetic coding, all the while sipping rum and muttering to himself: "I love you, Daddy. Thank you, Daddy. Daddy, why can't we all go to Harvard?"

He splashed more rum in his cup. "I love you, rummy. Nobody understands me like you do."

Two weeks ago, Pete and Paris entered the garage and set the genetic starter to percolate. Carbonated material arranged and sorted itself in the maze of pipettes wound through the nutrient regulator. Pete put an arm around his wife's shoulders.

"Congratulations, Missus Pendleton. You're a mother."

She stood on tiptoes to kiss his stubbled chin. "Right back at you. I was thinking maybe a purple layette this time. How would I look with violet eyes?"

And this morning, before Piper rushed into their room with demands of Xmasakah presents and breakfast, they hurried together to the garage with a purple and yellow baby blanket to greet the newest member of their family. Instead, they were greeted by a naked six-year-old sitting at the edge of the uterine accelerator picking her toes. It was Piper from the tips of said toes to the tops of her ginger hair. "Hi!" she said. "I fell asleep out here. Can I open my presents now?"

Pete and Paris exchanged parental looks. They'd expected acceleration, but nothing like this. Still, they opened their arms and their hearts, wrapped the baby blanket around her waist, and hurried her into the house to meet the formerly one-and-only Piper.

The proud, if perplexed, parents snuck her into Piper's bedroom where the original Piper snored and drooled on her pillow. Pete tenderly ruffled his daughter's hair. "Up and at 'em, sweetie. Merry Xmasakah."

Piper sat up in bed, rubbed her eyes, and at the sight of herself squealed, "Piper!"

"Piper!" squealed the new Piper in return, and they embraced, babbling and laughing, talking about puppies and the boys in the web-sims.

Pete and Paris stepped out of the room. Paris gave him a peck on the cheek. "I'll go make breakfast, and you …"

"... figure out what happened," Pete agreed. "But we did save a bundle on diapers."

His wife slapped him on the rump, and sent him on his way.

A few hours and a plate of organic soy chicken eggs later, he was in the workshop making his second pass at the accelerator coding when there came a knock at the door. Pete opened the door to a wide-eyed Paris, and Piper dressed in one of his Pre-Stained™ garage work shirts. "What's up?"

Piper smiled up at him, wrapped her arms around his waist. "Mama said I should ask you if it's okay to open my presents now. Can I? Pleeeease?"

He looked up at his wife, and then down at his daughter. "But you already did that."

"I found her in the garage sitting on the accelerator," Paris said, pulling herself together enough to affect a casual tone. "Her. I found her ... " Paris pointed at the smiling child. " ... sitting on the *accelerator*. We talked about how important it is to stay away from Daddy's equipment, didn't we?"

Piper, this Piper, Piper Number Three, had nodded, frowning with due seriousness. "Those aren't toys no matter how many buttons and lights," she'd said. Then she broke out in smiles. "So, can I open my Xmasakah presents now?"

Pete's stomach dropped to his feet; the eggs threatened to come up in the backwash.

Paris gave him a Do-something look.

Pete felt faint. "Yeah, I, um, sure, sweetie." I-can-fix-this his furrowed eyebrows said. "You go ahead. Daddy has some work to do out here, so, be good for Mama, okay?"

"Okay!" Piper ran off, a hapless Paris in tow.

Pete cut the power to the accelerator, forcibly

dismantled the replicator, left a dozen messages to a Maui number, and conducted eighty zillion-ish reviews of circuitry and quantum whozits. He read the instruction manual. Twice!

Too soon, Pete had eight Pipers upstairs, seven Pipers too many, making plans to dye the feather boa, and maybe Mama would let them dye their eyes to match. On the plus side, he'd given up panic in favor of drinking, and had made excellent progress on the bottle.

Another knock at the door, frantic and ringing with a hint of chipped ferro-enamel fingernails. Pete stopped drinking long enough to check the time. Half as long since the last knock. He blanched, and lurched to the door, not at all surprised to find Paris standing there, but damn near floored at the sight of two Piper's grinning happily. "Hi, Daddy!" they said in unison. "We fell asleep in the garage. Can we go open our presents now?"

He slid down the doorframe, staring up at his ... daughters? "Um, what? I'm sorry, I wasn't listening."

The girls climbed on him with hugs and kisses.

"Can ..."

"... we ..."

"... go ..."

"... open ..."

"... our ..."

"... presents ..."

"... now?"

One sentence in two voices, in perfect synch. Pete stared up at Paris who appeared to have left the building and not left her body a forwarding address. He rested his head against the wall. "Sure, girls, sure. Say hello for me."

Twice the arms, twice the hugs. "Okay!"

The Pipers dragged Paris off with them, leaving Pete

to contemplate the toes of his slippers. Brown slippers. Fuzzy brown slippers. Neither one named Piper. Lovely, lovely, lovely brown slippers.

Minutes later came a piping of Pipers from upstairs. "Piper!"

He crawled back to the desk and up into the chair. Not knowing what else to do, Pete poured the rest of the rum into his mug. He dialed the certified friend, who knew someone who was the friend of a friend and hung up at the "Sorry I can't take your vid right now, but I'm filming my son opening Xmasakah gifts. Follow me online!"

"Great. Just fricklin' great."

The pair, pair of them for God's sake, had taken half as long to form as the Piper before that. Something about that made a kind of warped sense. He gave up trying to get the computer to understand his perfectly reasonable diction, and dutifully typed in his numbers, peering at the screen with the vid flaw that made the read-outs wobble. Based on the hypothetical read outs, hypothetical because the thing shouldn't have frickling worked anymore, every Piper since the first had appeared in successively less time. "Just fricklin' ... great."

He closed his eyes, and opened them sometime later, no, don't tell him, just about half the time since the last Piper cleaners twins things, to find himself on his back and a concerned freckled face peering down at him. "Daddy, are you okay?"

He smiled up at his loving, perfect, whatever. "Just fricklin' great," he drawled, tousling her hair.

"Okay." She gave him a hug filled to the brim with six-year-old love. "I must have fallen asleep out in the garage. Can I open my presents now?"

"Sure. Can you, can you get Daddy a cray ... a cray ... a pencil marker thingy?"

Piper did, handing it to him.

Pete grabbed the wiggling thing with both hands. "Take off the cap, hmmm?"

Piper giggled, and did. "Oh, Daddy. Always bamfunning."

"Yup. That's me. Hold still."

She did, and Pete very carefully wrote "11" on her forehead. He took care to replace the cap. "G'won, sweetie. I'll be up … later."

"Okay! I love you." Another hug, and Piper skipped out of the room, leaving Pete to ponder the ceiling and his daughter's Xmasakah wish to hug the world.

Nor Tap in Time at School

"**O**kay," the writer says, scratching the back of her head with her pen. "Partridge and Pear Tree?"

A soft chirruping huff comes from the cluttered shadows behind her. She glances over her shoulder. "Good, good. Head on in."

The Pear Tree creeps up the ramp and through the portal of swirling black and white, taking the tiny Partridge with it. The writer marks them off her list.

"Two Turtle Doves? Has anyone seen ... okay, good. Head on in, guys."

Wing in wing, the birds strut up the ramp and step as one into the portal.

The writer paces before the ramp. Every now and again the toe of her right foot dips and skids along the poured concrete floor, causing a stutter in her step. "What about the French Hens? You're up next, Hens."

All agree, it's time for a rest. Turn out the lights, flip the sign, lock the doors, closed for the season. It's been a long year. Six months ago the writer's step was even without dip or stutter, then came the stroke, and therapies, and frustration. Now Christmas is coming, the doorway to year's end, and it's time to move on.

The hens mince forward, combs at attention, flags a flying. One chain smokes thin black cigarettes; the other two carry bottles of Chambertin. "Viva la France! Viva la France!"

The writer makes a note on her list. "Yeah. Viva whatever. In you go."

One hen stops and gives her a continental eye. "You are American, *oui?* Feh, Americans!"

The writer straightens her shoulders and salutes

with her pen. "Viva la Jerry Lewis."

"Viva la Jerry Lewis!" crow the hens, and they strut through the portal. The imagination is a quieter place for their passing.

Characters pack boxes and cover crates for next year, if there is a next year. The writer can't tell any more, and, like fistfuls of pills, the uncertainty makes her queasy. Once upon a time she might have splurged for vacation help, but times are tough all over. She rolls her shoulders against the stress of twelve days of overtime and no relief. "What's next? Have we got the Calling Birds? Golden Rings, you're up after the Birds."

From the rafters, four birds sound a challenge and flash down in a streak of bright feathers. The writer drops to her knees, clip board raised to protect her head. "Wait! I meant ... "

The birds swoop passed her, grab the five golden rings sitting on the edge of one of the crates, and carry them through the portal. A scattering of feathers float to the floor around the writer, tiny bits of emerald and amber. She sighs. "Um ... yeah."

Characters rush forward to offer help. "I'm fine, I'm fine," the writer says, perhaps more sharply than intended, and offers a thin smile in apology. She is tired of suffering for her art, but it's not the first time and certainly won't be the last. She crawls to the portal and pulls herself to her feet.

The geese go without too much fuss, their eggs rolling after them with ovoid enthusiasm. The swans won't budge until stagehands bring out the hoses and spray down the ramp. The runoff washes over their wide orange feet and soaks their bellies. "Cannonball!" says the last swan, and in he goes, wings wrapped around his knees.

The writer smiles at the silliness, somehow a reminder

that the year wasn't all bad. Trips to the park, dinners with friends, conventions, good conversations. She stifles a yawn and leans against boxes stenciled **UNICORNS** and **EXPERIMENTAL WAVE MOTION**. The writer flexes her right hand. The fingers tingle, though they aren't as numb as they were six months ago or even at the start of the shut-down. Some days are better than others.

Hospitalized. Six long months ago.

The writer frowns, rubs her face. Yeah, good times, bad times, worse times. The words don't come as easy since the stroke, sometimes don't come at all. She needs a rest, time away from the props, and dialogue, and metaphors. She'll be back, she hopes. She might take a walk, lounge in the tub, paint the den, walk the dogs. She snickers. Okay, maybe dream big and let someone else paint the den. In the end, what matters most isn't what she does, but that she takes time to recharge her batteries so she feels like writing again.

Time to get moving.

The writer cries with all eight maids, and laughs with six of the nine Ladies, the other three running up the ramp at the last minute. "Take care of yourself," one says, pressing an envelope into the writer's hands, and then she spins into the portal and slips away.

The writer works a finger under the flap. A copy of Robert Frost's "The Road Not Taken", and a gift certificate for an hour long massage. The writer tucks both at the back of her clip board. "Thanks," she says to the swirling portal. "Let's keep moving. Lords-a-Leaping, you're up!"

The lords leap, the pipers pipe ... and gift her with a hookah, no surprise there ... and last are the drummers.

"Drummers? Twelve drummers, you ready?"

No answer.

"Come on, guys. Rat-a-tat-tat. Twelve drummers, time to get drumming."

The other characters look surreptitiously around. The writer rubs the back of her neck. "Has anyone seen the drummers?"

Heads shake, murmurs in the negative.

"Great. Just great." The writer strides the length of the imagination, muttering her own negatives.

She finds the drummers standing around the only working water cooler. The horned men regard her approach with expressions of studied indifference.

The writer stops a few steps from the sweating cooler. "Hey, guys. How'zit going?"

The drummers shrug.

The writer smiles. "Time to get moving. You're the last to go."

"We're not going anywhere," one of the drummers says.

The writer opens her mouth, closes it. Tries again. "Pardon?"

"We're staying," says another drummer. None of their lips move. Like a high school percussion section, the drummers stand all for one and one for all.

The writer grits her teeth. "Okay. I thought we'd worked this out."

One of the drummers tosses his paper cup into the garbage, another snorts and spits. "Yeah, well, we changed our minds. We're tired of playing second fiddle."

"Twelfth fiddle," a Drummer mutters under his breath, and twelve voices snicker.

The writer pinches the bridge of her nose between her pointer finger and thumb, squeezes her eyes shut for a moment. "Come on, don't do this, okay. Last minute is always a bad idea. You know that, I know that, everybody here knows that. Let's just go through the portal and call it even."

A flat, hard: "No."

The writer inhales, exhales, does it again. "Okay. Okay. Help me understand. Why, all of a sudden, have you changed your minds?"

The click-snap of lights going out sounds in the distance, and another section of the imagination goes dark. Men, women, and things walk towards and beyond them, some nodding, most too busy to notice anything. The hum of the portal crescendos, softens. Pauses, and starts all over again.

"Like we said, we're tired to playing hind tit. Most people only pay attention to the first five verses of the song, anyway, and you did the same thing with your stories." The drummers fidget, claws rippling on snares, sticks rat-a-tapping on rims.

"What about my drummer story?"

"It sucks." With a cymbal rim shot.

The writer repeats her deep breathing. "I did my best. It was the last day, I hadn't slept well at all since I started, I was tired ... "

"That's just it," the Drummers say. "Everybody's tired by the time they get to us." A few threw their hands up in the air, others gave her wide, idiotic smiles. "Ooooh! Golden rings! Aren't they great? Wait. Isn't there something after that? Nah, who cares."

To a horned man, the drummers scowl. "So we're done. Finish your own drum solo, and leave us out of it."

The writer frowns, a slow burn creeps up her neck, her cheeks. "I really don't have time for this."

Two drummers shrug.

"So, what do you want?" the writer demands.

"Nothing."

The writer crosses her arms over her clipboard and chest. "No, I mean it. What do you want?"

"To be the first in the song for once."

The writer shakes her head. "Can't do that."

"Then we can't go through the portal." One, perhaps two, give her a single finger salute.

The writer paces back and forth with tight, impatient steps. Her right toe dips, she stumbles. "It's not my song. It's a traditional song, a helluva lot longer than ... look, why are we going through all of this again?" She stops and faces them. "I need you to get in the portal. Now. I'm on a deadline."

The drummers shrug. "Best of luck with that."

The writer throws her clipboard on the ground. "Jesus, for once in your miserable lives just do what you're told, okay?"

The drummers fill and pass out little waxed paper cups of cold water. "You heard what we wanted. Give us top billing, and we'll talk."

Lights click-snap. Voices call good-bye to one another, see you next year. Maybe.

The writer runs a hand through her hair, then bends in an exaggerated squat to pick up her clipboard. She stands with care, straightening the hips, the shoulders, finally the neck. She arranges the paperwork, the poem and gift certificate. "Are you sure this is how you want it to end?"

Drummers shrug a slow drum roll. "Ball's in your court."

"You got served," one adds.

Another ripple of laughter, a coarse, crude sound.

The writer looks beyond them, and nods. "Suit yourselves." She turns on her heel and walks away, calling as she goes: "The drummers are a no go. Let's get the rest of the similes sent out, and strap down the imagery."

Voices throughout the imagination agree, and an air of anticipation quickens the pace.

The drummers stay by the water cooler until the lights in their section are shut off, followed by others, and others, then the lights around the portal and beyond are shut down, and they are left in darkness.

"Um ..." says one.

"Is she coming back?" says another.

A third swears.

One at a time, the voices around them slip away,

fade to a sudden black and white stop. Silence follows darkness.

"Hello?" says one drummer.

"Shut up," says another.

"What if they left us here?"

"They won't." In the dark, the assertion doesn't hold the confidence it might once have.

"But it's dark."

"I said shut up!"

A stick skips across a skin head, clatters on the floor like a spider. "Who did that?"

"Um ... "

Emptiness follows silence, curling around it in a chill embrace. In the distance, darkness turns to nothingness.

"I don't think she's coming back."

"Sure she is. We just have to wait is all."

Darkness. Silence.

"It's, uh, really dark. You know, like, dark, dark."

The drummers nod, and cannot see the motion.

One of them swears.

"What?" demands half of them.

"Where's the water cooler?"

Silence. Emptiness.

"It was right here. Where did it go?"

"I don't ..."

"Will you knock off the ..."

"I can't find my sticks. I had them in my hand, and ... "

"Where are my feet?"

Emptiness.

"Wait for us!"

The drummers run as fast as they can in what they hope is the right direction, keeping haphazard time with hands and feet. Emptiness slips around them, coiling through their ranks, turning a dozen into eleven, into ten, nine, eight, seven, six, five, four, three, two, one ...

"Ready?" says a voice from everywhere at once. The writer.

The single Drummer stops dead in his tracks, scrapes the cipín across his bodhrán. "Wh-Who?"

"I said ready? We're all that's left, you and I, and I'm not long for this world. I really do need to rest."

The drummer whirls in a circle, looks high and low. "B-B-But the others ... "

"Are gone, like you will be once I leave. It gets lonely here after too long, and after the lonely leaves there's nothing. Nothing at all."

The weight of the last word trembles and sighs on the edge of a breath.

The drummer tugs on his horns and begins to cry. "But I'm ... and you're ... and I ... "

A portal of swirling black and white appears before the drummer. "Last chance. The others said no. It doesn't have to be that way. I don't want to leave you behind, but I can."

The drummer wipes his nose on his sleeve. "And ... and if I say no?"

Darkness. Silence. Emptiness. Or the portal.

The drummer takes a step forward, and the next, and the one after that. Finally, the little drummer boy of Christmas steps into the portal and disappears.

The writer folds the portal in half, quarters, eighths, on and on, until it fits snugly between the covers of a book which she slides onto the shelf.

She steps back, dusts off her hands, and smiles. "He's fine," she says. "The others are waiting for him under the tree, each the first verse in their own version of the song. I'm a bitch, but I'm not a *bitch*."

She winks at the reader. "Merry Christmas."

CPSIA information can be obtained at www.ICGtesting.com
Printed in the USA
BVOW07s1908121113

336129BV00001B/7/P